TRISTAN AND ISEULT

Tristan & Iseult

ROSEMARY SUTCLIFF

A Sunburst Book
Farrar, Straus and Giroux

CONTENTS

FOREWORD

To most people, the story of Tristan is only one chapter in a book about King Arthur and the Knights of the Round Table. But in fact it is a story in its own right, as old as the oldest stories of King Arthur, and like them, far older than any of the written versions we have today. And it only became joined on to the King Arthur stories quite late in medieval times.

The first written version that we know of dates from about 1150. Approximately ten years later, it was rewritten by a man called Thomas, and some fifty years later still, a great German poet, Gottfried von Strassburg, took Thomas's story and retold it in his own way. Since then, it has been told and told again down the centuries. Not much more than a hundred years ago Wagner made it into one of the great operas of the world.

In its far-back beginnings, *Tristan* is a Celtic legend, a tale woven by harpers round the peat fire in the timber halls of Irish or Welsh or Cornish chieftains, long before the time of chivalrous knights and fair ladies and turreted castles in which it is generally set. The medieval troubadours took it and enriched it, and dressed it in beautiful medieval clothes, but if you look, you can still see the Celtic story, fiercer and darker, and (despite the changes) more real, underneath. In this retelling I have tried to get back to the Celtic original as much as possible, and in doing this I have made one big change in the story.

In all the versions that we know, Tristan and Iseult fall in love because they accidentally drink together a love potion which was meant for Iseult and her husband, King Marc, on their wedding night. Now the story of Tristan and Iseult is Diarmid and Grania, and Deirdre and the Sons of Usna, and in neither of them is there any suggestion of a love potion. I am sure in my own mind that the medieval storytellers added it to make an excuse for Tristan and Iseult for being in love with each other when Iseult was married to somebody else. And for me, this turns something that was real and living and part of themselves into something artificial, the result of drinking a sort of magic drug.

So I have left out the love potion.

Because everybody else who has retold the tale in the past eight hundred years has kept it in, it is only fair to tell you this. I can only tell the story in the way which feels right to me in my own heart of hearts.

ROSEMARY SUTCLIFF

TRISTAN AND ISEULT

ONE

TRISTAN COMES TO
CORNWALL

*T*HERE was once a King of Cornwall, whose name was Marc, which in the ancient Cornish tongue means a horse—for which reason there was a story told of him that he had horse's ears. This was not true. He was a man like other men, and a warrior more than most.

When he was young, and new to the golden weight of the crown upon his forehead, there was war between Cornwall and Ireland, for the Irish had long harried the Cornish coast in their ships from across the Western Sea. Tidings of this war came to another King, Rivalin by name, in the land of Lothian. It was high summer, and it seemed to Rivalin that it was time his fighting men were blooding their spears again. So he called them together, and with his fine fierce company, took ship and sailed round Britain, which in those days was for the most part ruled over by King Arthur Pendragon, until he came to Cornwall.

Marc was joyful at Rivalin's offer of help, and they

turned together against the enemy from over the sea. The story does not tell how the war went, but it must have gone well for Cornwall, for when at last it was over, Marc gave his beautiful sister to the King of Lothian in thanks for the spears that he had brought into the fight.

Then Rivalin was glad, for he and the Cornish Princess had loved each other from the first moment that they met; and he carried her joyfully back with him to his own land.

For a year they were happy together, and then a son was born to them. But on the day that the baby came into the world, his mother the Queen went out of it. And the bells of all the churches of Lothian that had rung for her wedding, tolled for her burial.

For Rivalin it was as though the sun went from the sky and the world turned cold and grey about him; and for a long while he could not even bear to look at his son. He called him Tristan, which means sorrow. "Sorrow on my heart," said he, "that ever I went to Cornwall." And he gave him to the Queen's old nurse, who had come with her from her own country, and to the women of the Court, to care for. And then he turned himself back to ruling his Kingdom.

Seven years went by, and Rivalin took his son from the care of the women, and put him in the care of a young man called Gorvenal to train as a King's son should be trained. And Gorvenal, who loved him from the first as though he were a much younger brother, taught him to ride a horse and handle a hawk and a hound, a sword and a spear, to run and wrestle and leap. And from various masters, the boy learned other and stranger skills, which a hero must possess.

He learned the Feat with the Apples and the Feat with the Blades, the Feat with the Rope and the Feat with the Dart, the Feat with the Wheel and the Feat with the Shield-Held-Flat. He learned the Cat Feat and the Hero's Salmon Leap, the Feat of Swiftness and the Over-Breath Feat and the Hero Cry, and many more.

And from no one at all, but from deep within himself, he learned to play the harp so that it was as though he played not upon the strings of fine white bronze, but upon the very heartstrings of his hearers. And by the time he was twelve years old, there was not a bird in all Lothian but he could imitate its song so perfectly that any bird he called would answer him.

One winter's night when Tristan was sixteen years old, he and Gorvenal were sitting beside the glowing peats in Gorvenal's hearth-hall, the boy fingering his harp idly as though he thought aloud on it, the man with leather and waxed thread and blue-green herons' feathers beside him fashioning a new hood for his favourite falcon, for he held that every man should be his own falconer, and not merely fly the birds that other men cared for.

Tristan laid down his harp after a while, and sat staring into the fire, his chin in his hands and his dark straight hair falling forward about his face.

"What do you see in the fire?" said Gorvenal.

"I was seeing far countries," said Tristan.

And Gorvenal knew that the time had come to say the thing that had been in his mind to say for a while past: "Tristan, I too have been thinking of far countries. Here in Lothian you have learned all that we can teach you. There is no one who can outrun or out-leap you, no better swordsman, none who can wake the harpstrings as you can. Yet for a Prince to be fore-most among his father's subjects might be a somewhat easy glory, after all."

Tristan looked up quickly from the fire, and frowned, tossing back his dark hair. "I do not care for easy glory."

"That I know, for I know you. Well then, go to-morrow to your father the King, and ask him for a ship and his leave to go travelling, that you may see other lands and learn their customs."

So next day, Tristan went to his father. "Sir, now that I am sixteen and a man grown, it is time that I was learning something of the world beyond the borders of Lothian. I would see strange places and learn the customs of other lands, and try my honour against men who are not your subjects."

The King was glad when he heard this, and prom-ised Tristan the ship that he asked for, so that he might sail as soon as the winter storms were over. "And where will you go first?" said he. "You are free to go where you will, but I am a lonely man and you are all the son I have, and I should be glad to know in what land to think of you."

Tristan did not answer for the time that it might take a man to draw breath slowly; and then he said, "It has long been in my heart to visit my mother's country. My old nurse who came with her used to tell me long stories when I was small, of the land and the people, and the seas that beat upon its shores straight from the world's end. With your leave, I will go first to Cornwall."

"Cornwall brought me much of joy and much of sorrow," said his father. "Maybe it will do the same for you. It is a land not like other lands."

And Tristan said, "If so, I will count the sorrow as fair payment for the joy, my father."

So a ship was made ready and provisioned for the voyage; and when the sailing weather came after the winter storms, Tristan, with Gorvenal and a handful of young companions eager for adventure, set out on the long coastwise voyage. They landed on the southern coast of Cornwall, and bought horses, for they had gold in plenty with them, and rode northward for the Royal Stronghold of Tintagel.

"When we come to Tintagel," Tristan told his companions, "do not let any of us be telling who we are, for if I am to make a name for myself in the world beyond Lothian, I would do it by myself, and not because the King of Lothian is my father, and assuredly not because I am sister's son to the King of this country." And they saw his point, for they were all young and proud and hot-blooded themselves, and so they agreed; while Gorvenal, who was older, saw that there was good sense in the idea, and agreed also.

So they rode northward and northward, up river valleys and over bleak moors, until at last, on the evening of the third day, they smelled the sea, and came out from old dark oak forest and saw ahead of them a great turf and timber fortress standing high on a headland, with many long thatched halls and byres and barns huddled among sheltered orchards on the landward side of it, all hazed over with the smoke of evening cooking fires; and beyond it only the empty shining of the sea, with the great waves rolling in from the world's end, shot through with the gold of the sunset.

It was torchlighting time when they came to the strong gates of Tintagel, and the gate-guards passed them through, for no stranger was ever refused food and shelter there. And it was torchlight and firelight when they stood at last before King Marc in the Great Hall where he and his Court were already gathering to the evening meal.

And Tristan looked, and saw a big man with grey eyes and grey feathering in the dark of his hair, with a great hooked nose and a mouth like iron, and thought,

"Here is one with a gift for loving and a gift for hating, and when he hates, God help the man who earns his hatred."

And King Marc looked, and saw a stripling with grey eyes, straight hair as black as a chough's wing, and thought, "Here is a fighter's face and a lover's face, and there will always be fighting and loving wherever you are, my boy." But their hearts warmed to each other, though Marc did not know that they were kin.

The King bade them welcome, and beckoning to a short thickset man with the gold chain of a steward round his neck, bade him take them to the guest-place and see that they were fed, and treated with all honour.

But Tristan shook his head and said quickly, "My Lord the King, we thank you for your greeting, but it is not as guests that we come; we bring you our spears, to take service with you if you will have it so, and we would sit among your warriors at table and sleep among your warriors at night."

The King sat in silence a moment, his hands on the carved stallion-head foreposts of his great chair; and looked again from one to another of the young men before him. Then he said, "So. Most gladly will I accept your spear-service. But while a guest can come and go with no name asked and none given, I must know the names and country of those who sit at table and sleep at night among my warriors."

"We are all the sons of merchants from far off at the other end of Britain, who have no wish to follow our fathers' trades and so have set out to take spear-service instead," said Tristan. "I am called Tristan, and this is Gorvenal my father's steward, who like us, has little heart for trading. And this, Caerdin, and this Garhault. . . ."

And so he brought each before the King by their true names, and yet without letting him know who they were. And afterwards they went and sat among the King's warriors, and the platters of barley bannock and the great roasts of wild boar and deer-meat were brought in.

TWO

THE MORHOLT

*F*OR upward of two years Tristan and his companions were among King Marc's warriors; and as it had been in Lothian, so it was in Cornwall: there was no man who could outrun or outleap Tristan, or ride swifter on the trail of the roe deer, or master him at sword-play. King Marc's own harper could not make sweeter music; and he could throw any man in the Kingdom in a wrestling bout (and the wrestlers of Cornwall are famous to this day). There were some at the Court who were jealous of him; but for the most part he and his companions were liked well enough; and King Marc was glad of the day that had brought them to his gate.

And then a sore trouble fell upon the land; and this was the way of it.

The war with Ireland that had first called Tristan's father from Lothian, had flared up again a few years later. A peace had been patched together at last, but only on condition that Cornwall should pay a yearly tribute to Ireland in corn and cattle and slaves. Cornwall had paid the tribute for a year or two, and then both sides had let the matter drop. But not long before young Tristan came to Cornwall seeking his fortune, a mighty champion had arisen in Ireland; tree-tall and thunder-fierce with the strength in him of four men; and he married to the King of Ireland's sister. By the strength of his mighty sword that had been tempered in a brew of poison-twigs on the day that it was forged, he had conquered many islands and their peoples for Ireland. And the day came when he fitted out a fleet of ships and made ready to sail for Cornwall. He sent ahead to warn them of his coming, and that the time had come for paying the tribute that had not been paid for fifteen years. And he sent word that because the tribute had been so long owing it could not be paid in corn or cattle, but must be paid all in slaves; one out of every three children born in Cornwall in all those years. If they would not pay, then let them defend themselves as best they could in battle, unless they could find a champion brave enough to stand forth for them all and meet him, the Morholt, in single combat. A champion strong and skilled enough to defeat him.

When King Marc received the terrible message he called his nobles and his bravest fighting men together to Tintagel, and told them the choice before them; to give up into slavery one in three of all their children or to take on the might of Ireland in battle. No good even to think of a single champion; for what man, however brave, would go out against the Morholt who had in him the strength of four, knowing that if they failed to conquer him, as fail they must, they would have thrown away their own lives to no purpose at all?

Then there was a noise like a swarming throughout the land, and the warriors began to make ready for war, rather than yield up their children to be slaves. But in truth they had little hope of victory, for Ireland had grown very strong under the Morholt's leadership, with many conquered people to work and fight for her; and even as the men sharpened their weapons, the women wept and began to seek out places to hide their children.

Then Tristan went to the Lord High Steward, Dynas of Lidan, who had been his good friend since that first evening at Tintagel, when the King had bidden him take the strangers to the guest-place.

"It would be better than all this making ready for war, if we were to send the Morholt his champion," Tristan said.

"Much better—if we had such a champion to send."

"I will go out as Cornwall's champion, if you will have me."

"You?" said Dynas. "But you are only a boy! The Morholt would eat you alive!"

"I think that he would not. I have skills that you have not seen me use as yet."

"Tristan, do not be throwing your life away; this is Cornwall's sorrow and none of yours."

"Is it not?" said Tristan. "Yet go to the King, and make him promise that *who ever* comes forward as champion, no matter how strange or unlikely it may seem, he will not refuse them."

So at last Dynas of Lidan went to the King, and gained his promise. And when that was done, Tristan stood out before the King at supper in his Great Hall, with the eyes of all the warriors upon him, and offered himself as Cornwall's champion.

"You!" said the King. "But you are only a boy! To do as you ask would be to let you throw your life away!"

"I do not ask," said Tristan, "I demand that the King of Cornwall should keep his word!"

So word was sent to the Morholt that Cornwall would furnish a champion to meet him in single combat, after all. And back came word from the Morholt that he would accept only a champion who was his equal in rank.

Then King Marc sent for Tristan and told him this, half-grieving in his heart that Cornwall had lost her champion, half-glad that the young warrior who he had grown to love would not now be able to throw his life away.

But when he had done, Tristan said, "The Morholt is husband to the King of Ireland's sister, and indeed that sets him high; but would not the son of the King of Lothian and the Princess of Cornwall rank higher still?"

And then as Marc started up, staring at him, and scarce yet fully understanding what he had said, "When I came with my companions to your Court, I told you we were all merchants' sons, because if I was to make my fame in this land I wished to make it for myself, and gain your favour by earning it, not for the love that you bore to your sister, my mother; not because my father was your friend."

King Marc was silent a long while, and then he said, "This that you tell me makes it the more bitter hard for me to let you go to your death. But you have the right to stand forth as Cornwall's champion, and I cannot deny it to you."

So he sent the word back to the Morholt that a champion of the Royal House of Cornwall would meet him in three days' time, on a certain island just off the Cornish coast. But his heart was like a stone within him, for he was sure of Tristan's death.

At dusk before the appointed day, the King with Tristan and his foremost warriors and councillors came to the coast over against the island, and made camp there for the night. And far out to sea they could make out distant fire-petals that they knew were the stern braziers of the Irish ships. And at dawn they rose and broke bread all together; and King Marc served Tristan himself as though he was his armour-bearer, and put on him his own war tunic of fine grey ringmail and plates of polished bronze, and gave him a new sword that had never been blooded before, and a shield painted with a great black boar, and a red-roan horse whose saddle was of finest gilded leather.

Then Tristan led the horse on board the flat-bottomed boat that was waiting for him, and poled himself across the narrow strip of shallows to the island.

The Morholt was already there, and had moored his boat where the dark rocks and the hazel scrub came down to the water's edge. But when Tristan had landed and led his horse ashore, he pushed off his boat and let the water take it.

The Morholt stood holding his black horse by the bridle, and said when he drew near, "That was surely a strange thing to do, to push off your boat again, when you landed."

"Two of us are come to this island," Tristan said, "but only one will be needing a boat to carry him away." And they looked at each other long and straightly, each standing by his horse. And the Irish champion saw how young the Cornish champion was, and the clear battle-light behind his eyes. And something in his fierce heart said, "It would be a poor day's work to slay this valiant stripling."

So he said, "Surely this is a sorry thing, that we two who might well have been friends should seek to be each other's death. Is there no other way?"

"One," said Tristan. "That Ireland should forego this unjust tribute."

"Not that way. When I go from here the tribute goes with me. But between you and me—here is my hand in friendship, and the half of all I own—land and gold, horses and weapons, if you will choose to turn away from this combat, for I have no wish to be your death."

"Are you so sure you will be?" Tristan said. "Mount, and kill me if you may, and if I may I will kill you. That is all the peace that there can be between us."

So they went up to the level space at the heart of the island; and they mounted and drew apart to the furthest ends of their battleground, then wheeled to face each other.

Then Tristan struck spurs to his horse, and on the instant the Morholt did the same, and crouching low behind their shields, they thundered towards each other with levelled spears. They came together with a crash as of old bull and young bull when they battle together for the lordship of the herd. Each took the other's spear-point on his shield, and both spears were shattered into jagged shards. They cast the pieces from them and drew their swords, and fell to, hand to hand from the saddle. Tristan was the swifter swordsman, but in the Morholt was the strength of four men, and his blows fell so sure and fierce that the Cornish champion was driven back, and for a while there was little he could do but cover himself with his shield and defend himself as best he might. At last, in trying to guard his head, Tristan raised his shield too high, and the Morholt's sword came driving in under his guard

and took him in the thigh and laid it bare to the bone
so that the blood flowed out staining his horse's
shoulder crimson.

But it seemed as though the fire of his wound and
the red blood flowing that should have weakened
Tristan, kindled a desperate valour in him that he had
not found before, and with a yell, he wrenched his
horse round and crashed it into the Morholt's charger,
breast to breast, bringing horse and rider down together. The Morholt was up again on the instant, and
drove his blade deep into the breast of Tristan's horse,
which reared up screaming and then crashed to the
ground. Tristan sprang clear in time to see the Morholt's horse scrambling to its feet; the Morholt, lacking his helmet, had already a hand on the saddle and
his foot back in the stirrup to remount. Then strength
and speed such as he had never known before came
upon Tristan, and he leapt forward across the distance
between, and struck the Morholt on the wrist, such a
blow that his right hand with the sword still in it
dropped upon the trampled turf. His next blow took
the Morholt on the head, and bit so deep that when
he jerked out his sword a fragment of the blade was
left behind in the Irish champion's skull.

With a great cry the Morholt turned and fled, leaving a crimson trail down over the salty grass and black
rocks to where his boat was tied, and other boats from
the Irish ships were already putting in for him.

Tristan walked down to the landward shore of the

island, trailing crimson also through the furze bushes and over the grey shingle, to meet the boat that was putting off from the shore. Far off he could hear the sounds of the Cornish warriors rejoicing, but it was all hollow in his head, like the sea in a shell; and his blood soaked and soaked away into the shingle.

THREE

THE VOYAGE OF HEALING

*A*s soon as the ship that carried the Morholt
reached Ireland, messengers were sent for the King's
daughter, the Princess Iseult, for in all the land there
was none that had her skill in the healing craft. She
had all knowledge of physic herbs and their uses, the
secrets of spells to cool fevers and staunch bleeding,
and the ancient magic of the healer priests that men
would have called witchcraft if she had not been a
Princess. If she reached the Morholt while he lived,
she could save him; but even she could not bring a
dead man back to life, and by the time she had returned with the messenger, the Morholt was dead of
his wounds. Then seeing the piece of sword blade still
in his skull, she pulled it out, and laid it by, wrapped
in a piece of silk, in case she should ever meet a sword
blade lacking a piece that shape. . . .

Then all Ireland mourned for the loss of their
champion, and through all the length and breadth of

the land, the summer birdsong was drowned by the keening of women. And the King had the Morholt buried with great splendour, and gave orders that from that day forward, anyone landing in Ireland from a Cornish ship should be put to death.

Nevertheless, by the terms of the single combat, from that day forward Cornwall was freed of the tribute.

Meanwhile, Tristan had been carried back to Tintagel, and lay there with Gorvenal never leaving his side, while King Marc summoned physicians and learned men from far and near to tend him. But though they came, and looked at the terrible wound in his thigh, and applied this remedy and that, in the end they all shook their heads and went away again. "The wound was dealt by a poisoned sword," said they, "and we are powerless against the venom of such a blade."

So Tristan lay growing weaker day by day, and the poisoned wound blackened and festered and the smell of it grew so sickening that only the King himself and Dynas the High Steward and the faithful Gorvenal could bear to come near him. Then Tristan, loathing his own body and fearing even that he might spread some dreadful sickness through the Court, begged King Marc to have a little hut built for him on the seashore, where he could be alone with the waves and the seabirds, and be saved at least from knowing that his wound was making him a horror to other people.

So the little hut was built, down in the cove below the stronghold, where the black rocks cushioned with sea-pinks sheltered a little crescent of white sand; and there they carried Tristan on a hurdle, all the people following down the steep path from the headland, and mourning him as one already dead. And there he lay through the long days and nights, tended by Gorvenal and often visited by Dynas and the King. And as the days passed and the nights passed, so he grew weaker and nearer to death.

At last one day when the King came as usual, Tristan said, "I have been dreaming long dreams, lying here and listening to the waves and the seabirds; and it seems to me that any hope I have is out there on the waters. Lying here, I do but wait for death, without hope at all. It is time to cast myself on God, to bring me to the help I need, if there is help for me in this world. Therefore, will you do one last thing for me, my kinsman and my Lord?"

"I would cut off my sword hand for you, you know that," said Marc.

"I ask only that you will have a boat made ready, without oars or rudder, and set me adrift in it, with food for a few days. If God intends that I should find help and healing in this world, He will surely guide me to it. If not, then I had sooner die alone, out on the water, with the search still leading me, than here without hope."

"Not alone," said Gorvenal. "The boat must carry two."

Tristan shook his head. "Only a little boat. A boat for one. If I have not returned within a year, you must go to my father and tell him of my death and comfort him, and bid him from me to take you as his son in my place." And to the King he said, "Let you do as I ask. It is a small thing—a little boat, a little food, and my harp to carry with me; nothing more."

And King Marc bent his head into his hands and the salt tears trickled through his fingers. "I will do as you ask," he said. "But if you do not come back, I too shall have lost a son. Who shall comfort me?"

The boat was made ready and cushions spread in the bottom of it; and on the cushions they laid Tristan with his harp beside him, and food and drink for a few days. And again, folk gathered on the shore, mourning; and at the turn of the tide they pushed the boat out into the surf. For a long while it swung to and fro, and then the scour of the ebb tide caught it and swept it out round the headland into the open sea.

Soon Tristan was out of sight of land, alone with the waves and the sky. By day the seabirds swept between him and the sun, and at night the stars wheeled over his head; and he never knew how often the day turned to night or night to day again. But a dawn came when he caught the warm smell of land in the wind; and when, putting out all the strength he had, he lifted himself high enough to see over the edge of the boat, he saw that the tide was carrying him into the mouth of a great river. The sunrise shone golden through tall reeds, and wild swans beat up from the water with the light of it under their wings. And far off he thought he saw other boats, and farther still the smoke-haze of hearth fires. There was scarcely any strength left in him, and he knew that whether or no this was the place where he would find healing, his journey must end here. He had no strength to call, but he had his harp, and the old magic still in his fingers. He drew it to him and tuned the strings, and partly for a cry for help to any who might hear, and partly for the sunrise under the swans' wings, he began to play.

The skiff drifted nearer and nearer to land, and the men in the other boats saw it; a boat that seemed empty; yet as it drew nearer they heard wonderful harp music coming from it; and for a while they hung back, thinking it might be some kind of enchantment. But at last one or two fishermen bolder than the rest, brought their hide and wicker boats alongside; and when they looked down into the skiff, they saw a man lying there, all bones, with nothing of him as it seemed alive but his great fever-stricken eyes and his hands on the strings of a harp; and the stink of his wound all about him, and the music that he drew from the leaping harpstrings as sweet as the music of the Land of Youth.

And as they looked, one of the fishermen said to another, "Now was ever sweeter music heard in all Ireland since the Dagda himself would be putting men to sleep with the sweetness of his harp?"

And when Tristan heard them, his heart knotted up cold within him, for he knew well enough the orders of the King of Ireland. "It is a strange fate that has brought me to this place of all others," he thought. "And if these people find it is from Cornwall that I come, then indeed I shall find my death here." But his fingers never faltered on the harpstrings, and the fisherfolk did not dare to interrupt his playing with their questions, for the awe that was on them. But they put a line aboard the skiff and towed it in to shore, with Tristan still playing on his harp.

Now the King of Ireland was riding with some companions along the shore, and when they had brought the boat to land, one of the men ran and told him of the stranger they had found, for he was one who was interested in all strange and wonderful things. And the King came down to see this wounded stranger for himself.

And when Tristan saw him coming, he knew that it must be the King by the gold circlet on his head, and ceased his playing. And the King asked him who he was, and what had brought him to this evil plight.

"As to my name, I am called Pro of Demester," said Tristan, gathering all his strength to answer, and speaking the first name that came into his head, "and I am a minstrel, wandering the world. I was on my way from Spain back to my home in Brittany, when our ship was attacked by pirates—and in the fighting I got this wound, from which I think that I shall die. The pirates made me harp for them, and it seems that my harping pleased them, for they put me in this little boat, with food for a few days, and set me adrift to live or die as might be. And the days and nights that have passed since then, I do not know; but truly I think that they have killed me as surely as they killed the rest of those on board our ship."

"You shall not die," said the King, "for the world would be the poorer if your harp were stilled; and here in Wexford we have one who can heal any man who is not already dead." And he ordered his people to bring a hurdle and carry the stranger up to his Chief Falconer's house, for that was the nearest of the royal houses in the town; and he sent word to his daughter, the Princess Iseult, that there was a wounded man sorely in need of her healing art.

Now if the Princess had come herself all that happened after might have been very different. But she did not come. She questioned the messenger closely as to Tristan's wound, and when she had heard all that he had to say, she thought, "Clearly this is a wound given by a poisoned weapon, and all such wounds will yield to the green salve or the red salve or the black salve." So she made up the salves, and a soothing drink of herbs that break fevers and give quiet sleep; and she gave them to the messenger, saying, "Take these to the

Chief Falconer's house, and bid the ladies of the house to bathe this wounded man in cool water and give him the herb drink. And bid them spread the green salve on clean linen and bind it over his wound, and if within a day and a night it is no better, bid them do the same with the red salve; and if within a day and a night it is no better, bid them use the black salve and send to me; and I will come."

So the women of the house bathed Tristan in cool water and gave him the herb drink, and spread the green salve on his wound, and he fell into a long dark sleep; the first quiet sleep that he had known in many nights and days. And when he woke, the fever had left him, and the stink was gone from his wound as the green salve drew out the poisons and made the sick flesh clean and wholesome again. And when word was taken to the Princess that the green salve had drawn out the poison with no need of the red or the black, she sent healing herbs for the women of the house to use, and thought no more of the matter, for her healing skill was often called in use.

And so Tristan lay in the Chief Falconer's house, tended by his wife and daughters, while the edges of the wound drew cleanly together, until the day came when he was well enough to go his way. Then he took his leave of the Chief Falconer's household without ever having seen the Princess Iseult or she him at all. But the women of the Chief Falconer's household were sad to see him go.

He took his harp, and saying that one place was as good as another for a wandering minstrel, got himself taken aboard a ship bound for Wales; and from Wales he got another, and so came back to Cornwall long before his year was up, but long after Marc and Gorvenal and all who cared about him had given him up for dead.

FOUR

THE QUEST AND THE
DRAGON

*K*ING Marc was so overjoyed at Tristan's return, that he determined to make him his heir. But his Lords did not agree. "You are not yet old," they said, "marry and have sons of your own!"

"No son of my own could ever be as dear to me as Tristan," said Marc, "and none could ever be a stronger or a gentler King of Cornwall after I am gone. I have no wish to marry, for I am well enough as I am; and I have all the son I need."

At this, the Lords began to talk among themselves and some of them, who were jealous of Tristan, said that it was his doing, and began to look at him sideways under their brows. And Tristan, who had no wish to be King of Cornwall, heard their mutterings and saw their looks, and was hurt and angry in his heart, so that the next time they urged the King to marry, he joined himself to them, and spoke out more strongly than all the rest.

"My Lord and my kinsman, your nobles are right in wishing you to marry and beget a son of your own to rule Cornwall after you. And as for me, do you think I find any pleasure in knowing that the men I feast with and ride hunting with say behind my back that I am greedy for your throne?"

But even then, the King could not bring himself to agree at once. "Give me three days," he said, "and I will think deeply on this matter. And on the morning of the third day, come to me here, and you shall have your answer."

And for three days and nights he shut himself away and thought; but still when the third morning came, his mind swung one moment this way and the next moment that. Now, it was summer again, and he waited for the coming of his nobles in the open court before his Hall, sitting on a pile of fine crimson-dyed sheepskins, and playing with the ears of a favourite hound, while still he wondered what answer he was to give them. The swallows were darting under the eaves, and hearing a sudden thin twittering overhead, he looked up and saw two swallows quarrelling over something, darting and swooping in narrow circles and snatching the thing one from the other and back again. At last they dropped it, and as it drifted down, the King saw that it was like a thread of gossamer, yet not silver like gossamer, but red where the sun caught it, as hot copper. Scarce knowing that he did so, he held out his hand, and the shining thread drifted and eddied into it, and he saw that it was a long hair from a woman's head.

It was of such a colour as he had never seen before, so darkly red in the shade that it was almost purple, the colour of bramble stems when the sap rises in the spring, yet shining out when the sun caught it, bright as flame. "Surely," thought the King, "there can be only one woman in the world with hair this colour; and one woman in the world will be hard to find." And when a little later, Tristan and the rest of the nobles came into the forecourt, he showed them the hair and told them how it had fallen into his hand from the beaks of the two quarrelling swallows. "This is surely a sign," said the King. "And so now I give you my answer. I will marry as you wish, but only the woman to whom this hair belongs."

The Lords looked at each other. "There can be only one woman in the world with hair that colour," they said. "And one woman in the world will be hard to find." And again they looked at Tristan, sideways under their brows, believing that he must have put the idea into his uncle's head. Then Tristan stood forward from the rest. "My uncle, give me the hair, and a ship, and I will go and seek this woman, and if she lives, bring her back to you."

Then the King saw that there was no help for it; and he fitted out a ship with provisions for a long voyage and rich gifts for an unknown bride. And Tristan gathered a hundred warriors—Gorvenal the first among them—whose loyalty he knew he could depend on; and set sail to search all the countries of the world excepting Ireland, where it was still death for any Cornish ship to go.

Yet a man's fate is a man's fate, and none can wipe out the thing written on his forehead. The ship was caught by a great storm off the coast of Wales; and driven hither and yon as the winds and the waves beat upon it. There was neither sun by day nor stars by night to tell them the way they went; until at last the storm blew itself out, and they found themselves driven hard aground on a low reedy shore. And as the light grew, it seemed to Tristan that he knew this shore. . . .

It was the place to which his little boat had brought him in his search for healing!

They were driven fast upon the Irish coast below Wexford; and already he could see the fisher boats closing in in curiosity, and armed men spurring down towards them from the town. And with no chance of getting their ship off the beach before the tide rose again, they were trapped!

Then Tristan bade Gorvenal to bring a certain gold cup fashioned after the Breton style, that they had among the treasures on board; and when the armed band came spurring out through the shallows to the sides of the ship, and their leader, the King's Coast Marshal, demanded who they were and where they came from, he had a story ready for them.

"I am called Tantris, and I and my companions are merchants, from Brittany, where our wives and children are now. And we travel the world buying in one country and selling in another, and so make our living as honest men may. Two weeks ago we sailed with three ships from our home port on a voyage to Ireland, but off Lyoness the storm that has but now passed over, caught us and scattered us apart and drove us all ways at once, and last night it cast us here upon the Irish coast; but whether the other two ships were sunk or driven on some other shore, or whether they are still tossing on the sea far off from here, God knows. Therefore give us leave to land the horses which we have on board, for they are far spent with the pitching and tossing, and get our vessel farther up the beach where the tide will not lift her, while we seek for news of our fellows."

"How am I to know that you are not from Cornwall?" demanded the Coast Marshal. "My orders from the King are that the crew of any Cornish ship that comes upon these coasts are to be put to death without mercy. Can you give me any proof that you are from Brittany as you say?"

"Only this," said Tristan, taking the gold cup from Gorvenal, and holding it out. "You will see that it is of the Breton style."

The man's eyes flickered at the sight of the gold. But, "You say yourself that you buy in one country and sell in another. There is no proof in that," he said.

Tristan smiled. "Take it then as no more than a gift between friends, for yourself and your men. And play a friend's part to us, gaining for us the King's leave to bide here while we make our ship seaworthy again and seek news of our comrades."

And the Marshal took the cup. "I accept the gift in friendship, and I will speak for you to the King." And he went his way, leaving some of his men on guard.

"And what now?" said Gorvenal. "Think you that one will keep faith with us for the sake of a gold cup? Have you thought that he could break faith and still keep your bribe?"

"I have thought," Tristan said, "and it is in my mind that he is one who can be bought, but who will keep his half of the bargain. He has taken the cup, and if I read him aright he will help us in fair exchange. At the least, we have won a breathing space."

Now some of the bystanders came to help them get the horses ashore, and as they were splashing the scared beasts up through the shallows, the bells of Wexford began to toll, and the men looked at each other and one said to another, "That is the third time in as many days! You'd think they would be having more sense than to be still throwing their lives away on this hopeless business."

And the other said, "When a man is young, and the blood swift and hot within him, there's much that he will be risking for a beautiful Princess."

"Risk is one thing," said the first, "but to be going out against this fire-dragon is certain death, so it is."

When Tristan heard this, he was at once eager to know more. "Pray you, remember that we are strangers in these parts," he said, "and tell me more of this that you speak of—a dragon and a Princess and yon tolling bell—for I only half understand your words."

"Have you not heard, then," said one of the men, "of the sorrow that has fallen upon Ireland in these last few months? A terrible fire-drake is laying waste the land, and now that the Morholt is dead, we have no champion who is strong enough to stand against him. The matter is so desperate that the King has offered his daughter, the Princess Iseult, in marriage to any man who can kill the monster; and many bold young warriors have tried and failed. It is for the latest of them that you can hear the bell tolling now."

Then Tristan grew very thoughtful, and later, when the ship was safely beached above the tide-line, and the horses grazing under guard, he went below, and calling Gorvenal after him, bade him to help him arm. "I thought that would be the way of it," said Gorvenal, "for I never yet knew you to get wind of an adventure but you must be off on it! But truly this is madness! You heard what the men said—it is certain death to go against this fire-drake."

"It is I who got you all into this hazard, by bringing you with me on this strange quest for the Princess of

the Swallow's Hair; it is for me to get you out of it, if
that may be. —For if I should succeed in slaying this
monster, the King of Ireland can scarcely have us slain,
even if he discovers, after all, that we are from Cornwall."

"No, he will give you his daughter," said Gorvenal,
exasperated. "Have you thought what you will do with
an unknown Irish Princess, with this quest still before
you?"

"To be sure, there's the risk. And I value my free-
dom too much to wish for marriage yet," said Tristan,
laughing. "But who knows? She may be fair enough to
make me change my mind!"

And they looked at each other, and the exasperation
fell away from Gorvenal, and the laughter from
Tristan; and Gorvenal said, "At least take me with
you."

Tristan shook his head. "I leave you here in command. If in three days I have not returned, you must
give me up for dead, and get the ship re-floated, and
fight your way out as best you may; and God be with
you all. Now help me on with my mail and wish me
well."

And that night, when dark had fallen, Tristan took
his leave of his companions camped about the ship, and
while they made an uproar to draw the attention of
the guards, he got his own horse from among those
grazing on the shore, and leading it by the forelock,
stole away.

He found a thicket of hazels well back from the shore, and lay up there with his saddle for a pillow until morning; at first light, he mounted and rode off towards the hills where the dragon had its lair. He knew he was heading the right way by the scorched desolation of the countryside; and suddenly as he came towards the lower slopes of the hills, he heard a distant roaring, and across his path came a knot of mounted men, all riding as though the Wild Hunt was behind them; and as they passed, they shouted to him to turn back and fly for his life.

"Well, that makes my search easier," said Tristan to himself, and turned his horse into the track by which they had come. All the country looked as though a heath fire had swept across it; black snags of trees and bushes stood up from the ashy ground, and here and there among them lay the scorched and half-eaten bodies of cattle. The whole land reeked of death and fear. "Small blame to any that run from this place," thought Tristan, soothing his horse that had begun to dance and snort. And then, rounding an outcrop of heat-scoured rock, he saw before him a little hollow, and on the far side of it a cave mouth in the side of the hill. It must once have been a pleasant spot, where a stream meandered down through hazel bushes. Now the hazels were only black skeletons, and the stream boiled and spat like a witch's cauldron. And before the cave mouth, coiling itself to and fro in anger, was the dragon that he had come to seek.

It was long as a troop of horse, sinuous as a cat, and wicked as sin. Green bale light blazed from its eyes, fire and smoke and deadly fumes came and went, playing over it with the breath from its nostrils, and watching him come, it swung its upreared head from side to side like a snake before it strikes.

Tristan crouched low in the saddle, and levelling his spear, struck spurs to his horse and thundered down the slope towards it.

His spear point took it in the throat as it reared up to meet him, and tore its way in, wounding the creature sore. But Tristan and his horse plunged on into the heat and the poison-fumes, and crashing full tilt against the spiked and iron-hard breast scales, the horse dropped dead beneath him. Tristan himself sprang clear, and gained a moment's breathing-space, for the dragon turned on the dead horse, ripping and goring it instead of the living man. Then, with Tristan's spear still in its throat, it swung away, roaring in agony, and made for the rocks, uprooting bushes and scorched trees, and coughing out gouts of steaming blood as it went, with Tristan leaping after it with sword upraised.

Wedged under the overhanging rocks beside the stream, they came together again, sword against teeth and claws and flame. Tristan's shield was charred to cinders, and his ringmail seared his flesh as though he were clad in a garment of fire. But the dragon was weakening as the spear dragged at its throat and breast;

the lashing of its coils lost power, and its fire was sinking. And at last, seizing his chance, Tristan sprang in with his sword, stabbing deep, deep between the breast scales until the blade was engulfed to the hilt and the point found the monster's heart.

The dragon reared up with a bellow that was as though the heavens were falling upon the earth; its death-cry echoed to and fro among the rocks and the high tops of the hills and far out over the marshes, and as it crashed to the ground, its fire dying away, Tristan saw that it was dead. Gasping for breath and far spent himself with battle, he wrenched open its jaws, and with his sword, hacked off the venomous black tongue.

Then he turned himself to the wilds, meaning to lie up like a wounded beast through the day, and somehow drag himself back to rejoin his companions and the ship after nightfall. But his hurts were very sore, and it seemed to him that his body was still lapped in flame, and the world swam before his eyes and beneath his feet; and he all but stumbled into the stream where it came down toward the dragon's lair. It ran cool now, among the blackened tree snags and long trailing branches; it called to him, singing of coolness and rest; and he slipped into the water and lay down still fully armed under the bank, with only his head above the surface. And the water flowed through the links of his mail, hushing the parched pain of his wounds with coolness; and he slipped into a deep, black nothingness, half-sleep and half-swoon.

FIVE

THE PRINCESS OF THE
SWALLOW'S HAIR

*N*ow, one of the men who Tristan had seen flying
from the dragon's lair was the King's Steward, who had
long desired to marry the Princess Iseult, though she
had no liking for him at all. And when he saw that
Tristan went onward despite their warnings, he slipped
away from the rest, and turned back on his tracks. For
though he had not the courage to face the dragon himself, he most times contrived to be around when anyone braver than he went against the monster, so that if
by any chance they succeeded in the quest, he might
perhaps be able to claim a share in the killing. And so
he was near at hand when he heard the dragon's last
terrible roar; and he said to himself, "Nothing could
have made that sound, that was not in its death-agony.
The creature must be dead or dying! Courage now, my
heart, and we will see what there is in this for us!" And
he spurred his horse in the direction from which the
sound had come.

And so, searching among the rocks, he came upon the dead dragon and the torn remains of Tristan's horse, and the charred shield. —And of the dragon-slayer, no sign at all. "Surely the monster has eaten him," thought the Steward. "Ah well, he is not the first to be losing his life so; and if that is the way of it, his loss may be my gain." And drawing his sword, he fell to hacking away most valiantly at the dead dragon until the blade was bloodstained to the hilt. And then re-mounting his horse, he galloped away back to Wexford town, shouting that he had slain the dragon, and waving his bloodstained sword for all to see. He sent for a cart, and gathered his henchmen to return with him to cut off the monster's head; and when they had done so, and brought it in triumph into the town, he made for the King's palace to show him the blooded sword and grizzly hacked-off head, and claim the Princess's hand in marriage.

Now the King was torn between joy that Ireland was rid of the terror that had laid it waste so long, and grief that his daughter must be married to a man she loathed. But his promise had been given, and could not be broken.

So he sent for the Princess to come down to her betrothal.

The Princess sat at her embroidery, in her bower on the sunny side of the palace, and she heard the distant shouting as she stitched at the fine goldwork of a lily petal; and she said to Brangian, who was chief among her maidens, "Let you go and look from the window, and tell me why are the people shouting?"

And Brangian ran and looked, and said, "Someone has slain the dragon! There is a cart in the forecourt, and in the cart is the dragon's head! —Oh most horribly hacked and blood dabbled—and a man stands beside the cart with a bloody sword in his hand—and your father the King is there—and—and—"

"And the man with the bloody sword?"

"Oh my lady, it is the Steward!"

Now at this it was as though all the blood in the Princess's body sped back to her heart, leaving her icy cold; but she said, "There is some trickery here. I know the Steward; I know how little he has of courage. He could never have killed the dragon. —He is stealing some other man's glory."

And in that instant, there came the King's messenger, bidding her down to her betrothal!

The Princess set another stitch in the golden lily leaf, and said to the messenger, "Tell the King my father that I bow myself to his will, and I will come down to my betrothal, but not this evening nor yet tomorrow's evening, for I am weary and must rest. On the third day, when I have rested, I will come."

And when the man was gone, she said to Brangian, "Go to Perenis my cupbearer, and bid him have three horses saddled and ready by the side gate into the orchard an hour before dawn. We will be riding out and looking at whatever there is still to be looked at, in the place where the dragon was slain. There is some mystery here, and it may be that we shall find the answer to it." And she ran her needle into her embroidery so fiercely that it pricked her finger through the silk, and the lily petal was flecked with crimson. And she said, "We *must* find the answer to it; for rather than wed with that man, I will die."

Next morning, darkly cloaked and with their hoods pulled over their faces, the Princess and Brangian let themselves out through the small side gate into the orchard. Perenis was waiting for them with the horses, and they mounted and rode off toward the hills. They came to the valley, and found first the torn remains of the horse, and Perenis dismounted and bent over it to look at the harness. "This is such horsegear as I never saw in Ireland!" he said. And they rode on, following the signs of the struggle and found the headless body of the dragon lying among the rocks; and the Princess Iseult dismounted, and went close and looked at the spear in its throat. "This is not an Irish spear," she said. "Some stranger from across the sea has delivered Ireland from the monster, and it seems that death has been all his reward."

But it chanced that at that moment Brangian, who had wandered a little apart from them, glanced over toward the stream, and the morning sun, striking where it had not struck last evening, showed her a glint of bronze under the blackened alder branches. She called, "There is something—it looks like a helmet—over yonder in the stream." And Perenis and the Princess came running, and so they came all together down through the rocks and the alder and hazel scrub, and found Tristan lying in the water where he had lain for nearly a night and a day.

At first they thought him dead; but when they had dragged him up the bank and taken off his helmet, Iseult saw that he yet lived. "Quick!" she said. "Help me to unlace his mail and strip it off him, that we may see the wounds he has." And when they did so, they found him clawed as though he had been battling with a giant cat, and sorely burned from head to heel. "But given care, there is no death wound here," said Iseult, and she looked at the tiny packet of crimson silk that hung about his neck, and said, "We will leave it there. Maybe it is a talisman, or a keepsake from a maiden." And she took up another thing that had been thrust inside his mail, and said, "And this, I am thinking, by the look and the smell of it, is the tongue of the dragon that lies dead yonder."

Brangian said, "Dear mistress, you will not go to your betrothal to the Steward tomorrow."

"Nor any day," said Iseult, "nor any day." And she put the wet dark hair back from Tristan's bruised forehead and looked long into his closed face.

Then she and Brangian helped Perenis to lift him

on to one of the horses, and Perenis mounted behind him and carried him like a woman across his saddle-bow. And so they brought him back to Wexford, and into the palace, by the side door from the orchard, no man knowing of it, and up to the women's apartments, where they laid him on a bed, and the Princess began to tend his wounds as only she in all Ireland knew how.

Soon, like a swimmer drifting up from the darkmost depths of the sea, Tristan became aware of light above him, and soft voices and movement, and hands that touched him; and he opened his eyes and came back into the world. The light swam like water, but through it, he saw two women bending over him; and one had hair as black as the deepest moonless midnight; and the other had hair that glowed like hot copper, where the evening sunlight shone in upon it from an open window. And he thought, "Now whoever she may be, this is the maiden I came seeking, for surely no other woman in all the countries of the world can have hair of just that colour." And he moved his hand upward and felt the little silken packet about his neck, in which the single hair was safely stowed. The red-haired maiden looked from tending his wounds, and said, "It is quite safe. —And this also is safe, that we found stowed in the breast of your mail shirt." And she took up the silver bowl in which she had laid the forked tip of the dragon's tongue.

Tristan was so weak that his voice would barely

come. But he managed to answer her. "It is well for
me that you found and kept that wicked thing, for it
is my only proof that it was I who slew the dragon."

"It was for that reason," said the Princess, "that I
kept it with such care—and not for your sake, but for
my own. My father, the King, has promised me in
marriage to whoever can free Ireland of the monster,
and his Steward is claiming to be the dragon-slayer."

And then she knew what she had said, and flushed
as deeply as a foxglove, and looked away.

And Tristan said quickly, to cover her embarrass-
ment, "So you are the Princess Iseult. I should have
known, for I have heard that Iseult of Ireland is the
most beautiful of all women—and the most skilled in
the Healer's art."

"At this present time I am nothing but your most
grateful handmaiden," said Iseult. "And now I have
done tending your wounds, and you must drink some
broth, and then you must sleep. And while you sleep,
I will be your armour-bearer, and clean your harness
and your sword."

Indeed, sleep was already coming upon Tristan, and
when he had drunk the broth that she held to his lips,
he lay back and let it take him. And the last thing he
saw as he closed his eyes, as it had been the first thing
he saw when he opened them, was Iseult's face bending over him; but now the light had faded, and the
red of her hair had grown dark as brambles when the
sap rises in the spring.

When he was asleep, the Princess and Brangian took his armour and weapons into another room, so as to work without disturbing him. And while Brangian began to burnish his helmet, Iseult took up his sword and drew it from its sheath. There was a small piece broken out of the blade midway down. "This sword has seen hard service," she said; and she held it to the torchlight to see more clearly. And as she looked, it seemed to her that the shape of the small jagged gap was familiar. She laid the sword on the table without a word, and went to a carved and painted chest in the corner of the room, and brought from it something small and wrapped in silk. Coming back to the table, she unwrapped the packet and took out the splinter of iron that she had removed from the skull of the Morholt.

Very delicately, she held it to the gap in the sword blade—and it fitted perfectly!

Across the table where it lay, she and Brangian looked at each other. And a cold and terrible change came over Iseult's face. "It seems that the dragon-slayer is the slayer also of my kinsman, the Morholt," she said after a while. "And he is sick, and in my hands for killing or curing." And her eyes glittered like fire in ice.

Brangian, who was gentlehearted, cried out against her, "No! Oh no, my mistress!"

"Yes!" said Iseult. "Fate has given him into my hands, that I may avenge Ireland's champion."

"You cannot kill him! A man lying helpless at your mercy!"

"I can," said Iseult, softly. "But I shall not need to, I have but to show this sword to my father the King."

"And destroy the dragon's tongue! If this valiant warrior can prove that though he slew the Morholt he also slew the dragon, do you not think that the King must forgive him the one killing in return for the other?" Brangian said. "And oh, my Lady Iseult, remember, he is all that stands between you and marriage with your father's Steward! Is vengeance for a kinsman so sweet to you that you will pay *that* price for it?"

And Iseult was silent a long while, staring down at the sword on the table before her. "No," she said at last. "There is nothing, neither hate nor love nor life itself that I would pay *that* price for." And she began to laugh, shaking out her hair in a cloud of dark flame round her head.

So later that night she went to the King her father, and told him that the Steward was a liar and a cheat, striving to steal another man's glory and another man's reward; and that she had found the true dragon-slayer.

"As to that," said the King when he had heard her out, "here are two men both claiming the same kill, and who shall say which of them speaks truth? Their claims must be tried against each other; and I can give you no promise, Iseult my daughter, until that is done."

"Then let the trial be set for three days' time," said

Iseult. "The man I found is sore hurt by the dragon's claws and its fiery breath. And it will be three days before all my skill can make him ready to stand before the Assembly and speak for himself. But in three days he *shall* be ready, and he shall prove his right to the kill."

SIX

A BRIDE FOR KING MARC

$\mathcal{B}$ESIDE their ship, Tristan's companions waited for his return. And on the second day it was on all men's tongues all up and down the river, that the King's Steward had slain the dragon, and that an unknown warrior who had gone against the monster before him had been slain and devoured. And Tristan's companions looked at each other, and their hearts sickened within them. Then Gorvenal flung on a rough dark cloak such as would blend into the countryside, and slipped away, heading for the dragon's lair. He found, as the Steward and the Princess had done, the headless dragon and the torn remains of Tristan's horse and his blackened shield; and he went back to the ship, his heart like a stone in his breast, and told the others what he had seen.

"Then it seems there can be no hope that Tristan is still alive," said one of the Cornish warriors. "Now we must make ready to get the ship to sea, and save ourselves as best we can."

But the men who had followed Tristan from Lothian said, "Gorvenal could not find him living, but has not found him dead; and if in truth by some chance he still lives, it would be a sorry thing if we were to leave him to his fate."

"A warrior was slain by the dragon on the day that Tristan went upon this quest," said another of King Marc's Cornishmen, "and surely, if he yet lived, he would have returned to us by now."

Gorvenal stood and looked them over; and those who were for putting to sea felt as though an east wind were blowing when he looked at them. "Three days, Tristan bade us wait for him, and we have waited but two. Therefore we will wait at the least another day, and one more after that; lest he has been delayed yet still comes. If you warriors of Cornwall leave now you will leave without me, and the men of Lothian will bide with me; and you can explain as best you may to King Marc, how it is that you return without us, as well as without Tristan."

And so, seeing that there was no help for it, the others gave way; and the ship waited for Tristan still.

And in that same hour, two things happened. The King of Ireland let it be known that another warrior had claimed the dragon-kill, and that his claim and the Steward's would be tried on the third day; and Tristan, gathering all the little strength he had in him, wrote a message to Gorvenal, telling him what had happened, and bidding him and the rest of the company to be present at the trial; to come in the best and bravest of the garments they had on board, and bearing themselves as befitted bold and honest merchants of Brittany. And this he did because no one in Ireland, as he thought, knew that he was anything but what he had claimed to be, a Breton merchant, and his companions likewise.

When they knew that Tristan was alive after all, the men of Lothian set up a great shout of rejoicing, and the Cornish warriors forgot that they had ever been for putting to sea without him, and rejoiced also. And they set to bringing out their gayest clothes and burnishing their weapons, to do him credit at the trial.

The day of the Assembly came. It was to be held in the great timber Hall built on a mound in the middle of the town, where the King held the great three-yearly gatherings of his clan chieftains, and gave justice, and feasted the embassies of foreign lands. Such a Hall as the King of Ireland had had from the days of Conor MacNessa; lightly built as a hunting booth, but hung inside with blue and purple and crimson, its timbers painted, its floor strewn with fresh rushes and water-mint and the starry blued-eyed grass. Here, the foremost of the King's chiefs and nobles were gathered, and here too, the merchants from the Breton ship in the river, not looking quite like merchants but rather as though they were warriors and nobles also. And the eyes of every man in the place were upon the terrible dragon's head, on its cart that had been dragged in through the wide doorway and stood beside the central hearth.

Then the King entered in the midst of his body-guard, and seated himself in his High Seat that had the skin of a black bull spread over it. And after him came the Princess with her maidens, walking proud under the royal circlet that bound her hair, and took her place on the pile of embroidered cushions at her father's feet. And then there was a rustling and a wait-ing, and the Horn of Summoning sounded, and from the door on the right of the Hall the Steward strutted in; and from the door on the left came Tristan, still weak from his wounds, but carrying himself so that men whispered to each other, "This is no merchant, but a King's son!"

And Tristan looked at no man, but at the dragon's head beside the hearth, and he wore his fighting face under the silken surface of good manners.

Then the King struck the forepost of his chair with the silver rod in his hand, for silence. And in the silence, he spoke. "Chiefs and nobles of this land, I have called you here today on a matter that concerns you as it concerns all Ireland, as concerns Iseult my daughter and your Princess. You all know—how could you not?—of the hideous dragon that of a sudden came upon us, and of the havoc and desolation that it has

wrought in these past few months. You all know that
in despair I offered the hand of the Lady Iseult, being
the greatest treasure that I have to offer, to any man
who could rid the land of this terror. You all know
how many of our boldest and most valiant warriors
have died in the attempt. And now the terror is ended;
you see the dragon's head lying here before you; and
two men claim the honour of the kill. Therefore I call
upon them both to give proof of their claims; and
since my Steward was the first to name himself the
dragon-slayer, let him be the first to speak before this
Assembly."

Then all men looked toward the Steward, who stood
forward boldly enough. "My Lord the King, I can but
say once more, before this Assembly, what I have said
before. I did indeed slay the dragon, I and no other
man; I slew it after a long and bitter struggle, for the
love of the Princess Iseult. And here in this cart lies
the monster's head to prove my claim as clearly as
though it could speak! What better proof could there
be than that?"

"I can think of better," said the King. "A man
might—he just might—come upon the carcass of a dragon slain by another man, and cut off its head, thinking to claim the kill."

"And what man would slay the dragon and walk
away?" demanded the Steward.

"Let the second man to claim the kill answer that,"
said the King.

So Tristan stood forward also, and gave the Steward back look for angry look. "My Lord King, although a merchant, I have some skill with weapons; and hearing of the sorrow of Ireland, and thinking that if I could slay the monster it might be good for the trade, I went out against the creature and by God's Grace slew it, but being sorely burned by its fiery breath, when the slaying was over, I crawled away to cool my wounds in a nearby stream, and there a great blackness came upon me. And it must be that while I was lost in the blackness, this man came and found the dragon, and thought his way clear to the reward that another man had done the work and the bleeding for."

"Lies! All lies!" cried the Steward. "Look at the monster's head! My sword is yet blackened with its blood!"

"Then you should see it cleansed," said Tristan contemptuously, "a good sword deserves better treatment than that, Sir Steward!" And added for good measure, "But it was a good thought, to blood your blade on the carcass."

"Liar!" The Steward was crimson with fury, his eyes standing out in his head.

"One of us is a liar indeed," Tristan said. "But it is not I."

Then the King spoke again, while the Princess looked on and played fiercely with the gold bracelets on her arms. "Will you submit to trial by single combat, leaving God to show who is the liar?"

At this, the Steward turned from red to grey and said not a word; and Tristan said, "By God's Grace, I have no need to foul my sword on the like of this creature, for I have another way to prove that I speak truth. —This head has been closely guarded?"

"Night and day," said the King.

"None could have come near it unknown, since it was hacked from the body?"

"None," said the King.

"Then let some of your men force open its jaws. Maybe it could have spoken, to prove your Steward's claim, *if it were not lacking the tip of its tongue!*"

It took four of the Irish warriors, using all their strength, to force the great jaws open, and when they did so, there in the bloody cavern of its mouth, clear for all to see, was the black stump of the tongue!

Then Tristan sprang up into the cart, and took from a folded napkin that he had been holding all this while the leathery forked tongue-tip. "My Lord the King, is the proof enough?"

"The proof is enough," said the King.

And when they looked round for the Steward, he had slipped away!

A sudden gale of laughter went roaring through the Hall. And before it was quite silent, Tristan dropped the dragon's tongue beside its head, for it had served its purpose; and leaping down from the cart, went and knelt before the King. For he knew that the next thing must be done quickly, while the King and every man in the Hall was on his side.

"My Lord of Ireland, there is a thing that I must tell you now, lest you should hear it in another way, and harm should come to two Kingdoms thereby."

"And what is this thing?" said the King.

And the Princess Iseult looked up quickly between the long red curtains of her hair.

"It is this," Tristan said. "Four days since, it was I who slew the dragon. Two years since, it was I who slew the Morholt."

There was a frozen silence, and a long gasp ran through the Hall where lately the laughter had been; and the Princess Iseult twisted the bracelet on her wrist until it made red weals on the white of her skin.

The King's brows drew together until they all but met. "You? You killed my kinsman, Ireland's champion? Do you know what it is that you say? That you dare to say, standing here before me and among my warriors?"

"I do," Tristan said. "But let you bear in mind, my Lord the King, that it was not done in the dark, or by an arrow in the back, but in fair fight, his life or mine; and that the challenge was his."

"That is true," said the King slowly. "And it is true also that you are no Breton merchant. The Morholt was slain by Tristan of Cornwall."

"I am Tristan of Cornwall," Tristan said proudly.

"Sister's son to King Marc. And these my companions are Cornish nobles, save for twenty, who came with me in the beginning from my father's Kingdom of Lothian. We had no thought to come to Ireland, knowing that it was death for any Cornish ship. But a man's fate is his fate; we were storm-driven upon your coast, and being mortal men we had sooner live than be slain, so we told the best lie we could."

"What were you doing in our seas at all?" said the King.

"We were making for Wales when the storm took us. Yet truly, fate was in that storm, for we were bent upon a certain quest, and we could never have found what we sought, save here in Ireland, after all."

"You speak in riddles," said the King.

"I will make them plain." And Tristan told the whole story of the quest for the Princess of the Swallow's Hair.

"So then," said the King, when he had done, "if I give you the Princess Iseult, you will take her, not to be your Lady, but to be Queen of Cornwall."

"That is so," said Tristan, and he turned his head to look at the Princess, but she never looked at him. "It was for that, that I took this quest upon me, little thinking that it would lead me here."

"There has been little friendship between Ireland and Cornwall these many years past," said the King, "that I should give the Lady of Ireland to be Cornwall's Queen."

"It would bring peace between the two countries, and would that be so bad a thing?"

Then the King of Ireland thought for a long time, with his chin in his hand. At last he said, "After these months since the dragon came upon us, truly we are in no case to be at war. Maybe it is time that friend-ship came between Ireland and Cornwall; and it was Fate indeed that flung you upon these shores. . . . As for King Marc, I have heard no ill of the man. So, take her, then, not for yourself as is your right, but for your King. And for the other matter—it comes hard on a man of my race to turn his back on a blood-feud for slain kin, but I must count the dragon's death as fair and full payment for the slaying of the Morholt. So, when you go from this place, go in peace, and carry the peace between our two lands with you."

So Tristan had ended his quest, and found for King Marc of Cornwall the Princess of the Swallow's Hair. But in all that morning in the Royal Hall, Iseult of Ireland never looked at Tristan, nor spoke one word.

SEVEN

THE HIDDEN VALLEY AND
THE MORNING TIDE

*T*HERE were days of merrymaking at the King's Court, hunting by day and feasting and harping by night, while Tristan's ship was made ready for sea, and another greater and finer vessel prepared to carry the new Queen of Cornwall to her Kingdom. But among the Irish, the merrymaking fell away and the harp-songs took on a sadder note as the day for losing their Princess drew near.

And when at last the time came, and the two ships lay ready to sail on the morning tide, not only the King and the Court, but as it seemed half the people of Ireland followed her down to the harbour. Many of them were weeping; but the Princess walked in their midst, with her head held high, like a lily under her goldwork crown; and never a tear in her eye.

So she took her leave of her father, and went on board with Tristan, Brangian and her maidens, and Perenis her cupbearer following after. The sails were broken out from the yard, and the rowers bent to the oars, and they slipped out of Wexford harbour on the morning tide.

It was fair sailing weather when they started out, but by evening the wind and the seas were rising, and the ships began to pitch and toss. And down in the single cabin that had been made for them in the space below the deck, the Princess's maidens were sick and afraid. Tristan, going to see how they did, found them holding their heads and groaning; but the Princess sat on cushions with her back against the mast, and stared straight before her into the heaving shadows, as silent as she had been before the Assembly in her father's Hall. Yet it was the Princess he was most troubled for; and he went back to the Shipmaster, and said, "If the seas do not run softer by morning, I am thinking that we had best run for shelter somewhere along the Welsh coast."

At dawn, the seas were running as high as ever, the rowers were fighting the oars, and the salt spindrift flying back along the deck. And when Tristan went below again, Brangian and the other women cried out to him to know if the ship were sinking, and prayed it might be. But the Princess still sat on her cushions against the mast, staring before her into the shadows.

"How is it with you, Lady?" Tristan asked.

"As well as with any woman torn from her home to wed with a man she has never seen and rule with him over a strange land."

"You could have stayed in your own land and wed with your father's Steward," said Tristan, stung by her tone. "The choice was in your hands, Lady."

And she said, "I had rather die," and still stared straight before her.

"We shall all die," said one of her maidens, moaning and pulling her cloak over her head, "and for me, unless we find harbour soon, drowning cannot come too swiftly."

And Tristan went back to the Shipmaster and said, "Where is the nearest shelter that we may make for on the Welsh coast?"

"There's a cove I know of well, that we could make by noon," said the Shipmaster.

So the two ships parted company and while the smaller, with Gorvenal in command, beat on for Cornwall, the other, with Tristan and the Princess on board, came about in a sea-swallow curve and sped away before the wind toward the dim blue hills of Wales.

At noon they came under the shelter of a long low headland of dunes and soft shore grasses and dark, yellow-sparked gorse, and instantly the water gentled. They dropped anchor in the little cove, where a stream came down from the hills through a steep valley where elder trees were in flower, and the song of larks and the warm scents of the land mingled with the crying of gulls and the cold salt smells of the sea.

The rowers shipped their oars, and the ship lay rocking gently with furled sail, and the Princess and her maidens came up from below and looked with eager eyes toward the land. Then Tristan and others of the men sprang overboard into the shallows to carry the women ashore. And Tristan held up his arms to the Princess as she came out over the side, and caught and carried her up through the shallows, so that when he set her down on the white wave-patterned sand, not even the soles of her shoes were wet.

Now this was the first time that ever they had touched each other, save for the times when the Princess had tended Tristan's wounds, and that was a different kind of touching; and as he set her down, their hands came together as though they did not want it to be so quickly over. And standing hand in hand, they looked at each other, and for the first time Tristan saw that the Princess's eyes were deeply blue, the colour of wild wood-columbines; and she saw that his were as grey as the restless water out beyond the headland. And they were so close that each saw their own reflection standing in the other one's eyes; and in that moment it was as though something of Iseult entered into Tristan and something of Tristan into Iseult, that could never be called back again for as long as they lived.

But they pulled their hands apart before anyone, except Brangian, had noticed anything at all.

Before evening Tristan and his companions built a little branch-woven hut for the Princess, of hazel and elder boughs with the blossom still upon them, away up the valley where the little stream came down; and they brought up rugs and cushions from the ship to make it fair and pleasant for her and Brangian. And for the other maidens they built a hut lower down the valley. And the men slept beside the ship, down on the shore.

When morning came the sun shone and there was shelter in the little cove under the headland; but out beyond, the seas ran swift and grey, and flecked with the white crests that men say are the manes of Manannan the Sea God's horses. And Tristan said to the Shipmaster, "We must wait another day for the seas to gentle." But in his heart he was glad, for the gorse was honey-scented in the sun, and he had lain awake all night, watching the glimmer of light from the little cabin up the stream side.

But he did not seek out the Princess Iseult; he wandered off by himself and lay in the warm sand on the sheltered side of the headland, with the sea wind blowing over, and let the sand trickle through his fingers, and watched the grass bend and shiver along the dune crests, and the tiny pink creeping flowers of the Restharrow. And it was the Princess Iseult who came seeking him, with a little packet of yellow silk in her hand, and found him there.

She said, "Since you carried me ashore yesterday, you have scarce spoken to me nor looked my way."

"Lady," said Tristan, "you were a most gentle physician to me while I lay sick of my wounds; but since then, it has not seemed to me that my company was pleasant to you."

Then she was silent, looking at him a while. She had loosed her hair from its braids so that it blew freely about her head and the sun and the sea wind played with it. But Tristan looked beyond her, out to sea. At last she said, as one making up her mind, "I have brought something to show you."

And she unrolled the little packet of yellow silk, and held out to him on the palm of her hand a splinter of iron, jagged along one edge and sharp as a sword blade along the other. And Tristan looked at it, and then at her, not yet understanding.

"Draw your sword, Lord Tristan," she said. "Draw your sword that I burnished for you when you lay sick."

And Tristan drew his sword, and she fitted the splinter of metal into the gap in the blade.

They looked at each other, with the sword lying naked on the sand between them. "So you knew," Tristan said at last, "before ever I told your father that it was I who slew the Morholt; all the while that I lay sick, you knew."

"I knew," said Iseult.

"Why did you not avenge your kinsman? You who know so much of healing herbs must know much also of those that kill. —Or you had only to tell the King your father, before I had the chance to prove to him that if I had slain the Morholt I had also slain the dragon. It would have been easy to kill me, Iseult."

"It would have been easy," said Iseult. "But I would have had to marry my father's Steward. And remember, I thought then that the choice was between him and you, not between him and a stranger King."

"I am glad at all events," said Tristan, "that for that little while, I pleased you better than your father's Steward." And it was as though they were fencing, with words for weapons, neither saying the thing that was real in their hearts.

"You pleased me well enough," said the Princess. "And then I found that it was not you at all, but only the King of Cornwall who must please me." And she tossed the splinter far away into the dune sand, as a thing that was now of no account. "And what difference does it make, after all?"

And Tristan looked up from sheathing his sword, and found her still looking at him, and said, "What is it that you want of me, Iseult?"

"Nothing," she said, "nothing in this world or the next." And she turned and walked away.

That evening the light glimmered again from the little branch-woven bothie up the stream side; and Tristan looked often towards it as he wandered restlessly to and fro on the edge of the camp. At moonrise the Shipmaster came to him and said, "The wind has gone round and already the seas are gentling; it will be fine sailing weather tomorrow."

"Then have all ready to sail on the morning tide," said Tristan, and he sent young Perenis to warn the maidens in the lower hut, but he went himself up the stream side toward the light of the Princess's bothie, to tell Iseult himself. And at every step something within him shouted to him to turn back and send Perenis to the Princess also, but still he went on.

They had hung a cloak over the doorway, but it was flung back, for the night was warm as milk; and the Princess and Brangian were sitting on cushions combing their hair, the red and the black together, by the light of a honeywax candle. And as he came to the doorway, Iseult looked up and bade him enter, and Brangian got to her feet and slipped out.

"I hoped that you would come," said the Princess Iseult, "for there were things that I would have said to you today out on the headland, that I did not say."

"I came only to warn you that the seas are gentling and tomorrow we must sail with the morning tide. In two days, Lady, if all goes well, you shall be in Cornwall."

The Princess stopped combing her hair. "I would that the seas might never gentle, and I might never come to Cornwall," she said. And she made room for Tristan on the cushions where Brangian had been, and he came closer and sat down at her side.

"Lady," he said, "the same thought is in my mind; but it is best forgotten. You will be happy when you come to Cornwall, and King Marc my kinsman will be a kind and loving Lord to you."

"Kind he may be, and loving he may be, but that is not what will make me happy; for I do not think that ever I shall be happy again," said Iseult. "This is the last day that ever I may be happy on, and already the moon is up."

And when he made no reply, she said, "Shall I tell you the true reason that I did not kill you when I found the splinter lacking from your sword blade?"

"I am thinking," said Tristan, "that it is best you do not tell me."

"It was because I loved you," said the Princess. "I was not knowing it then. I was not knowing why it was like a sword turning in my heart when you stood before my father and claimed me for the King of Cornwall when I had thought to hear you claim me for yourself. I was not knowing until you lifted me in your arms to carry me ashore in this place. Tristan, whoever takes me for his wife, whether you will or no, and God help me, whether I will or no, you are my Lord as long as I live."

And Tristan bent his head into his hands and groaned.

"Do you love me?" said Iseult.

And Tristan felt as though his heart were tearing in two within him. "Iseult, I am King Marc's man!"

"But do you love me?"

"And I owe him all my loyalty."

"This man-talk of loyalty means little to me," she said. "Love matters more. Do you love me?"

And Tristan said, "I love you. Though it is like to be the death of both of us, I love you, Iseult."

And he sprang up and turned to the doorway; but she was before him. "Then stay here, and be with me a little while, before we lose each other."

So Tristan put his arms round her and held her fiercely close, and she clung to him so that they were together as a honeysuckle clinging to a hazel tree.

But when the night was over, they sailed with the morning tide.

EIGHT

THE BRANCH IN THE
STREAM

WHEN they came to the landing beach below Tintagel, Iseult of Ireland stood in the bows of the ship, wearing her most brilliant gown, and the royal goldwork in her hair; and Tristan stood beside her, ready to lead her ashore. Their ship had been sighted from afar by the lookouts on the high castle headland, and King Marc, who had known of their coming since Gorvenal reached him with the whole story two days before, had come down to the landing beach to greet his bride, the Princess of the Swallow's Hair.

And when the ship came to rest beside the timber jetty, and Tristan took Iseult's hand to aid her over the side and lead her to where the King stood waiting, it was as cold as ice.

King Marc looked down at her, and said, "Until now, I thought this marriage would be for the binding together of an old rift between Cornwall and Ireland, but now I know that it is also for making music in my heart." And he took both her hands between his own. "Your hair is as red as flame, but your hands are so cold. Yet mine are big enough to warm them." And he stood looking down at her a moment, before he drew her to him and stooped his head and kissed her.

And Tristan, turning aside to greet old friends and old enemies, thought, "He loves her too! Dear God in Heaven, the King loves her too!"

Eighteen days later, King Marc and the Princess were married. Iseult was no more Iseult of Ireland but Iseult of Cornwall; and her place was beside the King, and the gold circlet of a Queen was on her head. And for a long time, or it seemed a long time to them, Tristan never looked her way nor she his; and the old bond between Tristan and the King his uncle was as it had been before.

So all the autumn and the winter went by, and the year turned back to spring, and then one day when the gorse was in flower along the headlands, Tristan came upon the Queen in the little garden that clung to the rocks below the castle; and she was looking towards Ireland and weeping. And all his love for her that he had pushed far down into his dark and deep-most place, came rushing up to the light again; and he put his arms round her and held her close and kissed her as he had done in the little hut among the elder trees. And after that there was no going back for either of them, to where they had been before.

As ill-fortune would have it, they were seen by

another nephew of the King's, Andret by name, who was jealous of Tristan. And from then on, Andret spied upon them until he was sure; and then he went to the King and told him that there was love between Tristan and the Queen.

The King would not believe him. "You have always been jealous of Tristan since first he came from Lothian," he said.

"I do but tell you the truth, for I cannot bear to see you so wronged."

"You could bear very well to see me wronged," said the King. "You do but tell me what you think will harm Tristan in my eyes. Tristan has proved his faith to me in a score of ways, he is the champion of Cornwall, and it was he who brought my Queen to me in the first place—"

"How do you know what they were to each other before ever he gave her into your hands?"

"—and I will not believe ill of him unless I see the thing with my own eyes."

"But if you do see the thing with your own eyes?" said Andret, eagerly.

"Then I will believe, and not till then."

And the King set his mind against what Andret had told him, and swore in his heart that he would not watch his wife nor Tristan, the two people he loved best in the world. But despite himself, it was as though Andret's words had pulled some kindly mist from before his eyes, and he began to notice the glances that passed between them across the Hall, and the way Iseult grew still at the sound of Tristan's voice. And then one day, coming quickly into the women's apartments, he found them with their arms round each other, and Iseult's red hair falling all about them both. And they sprang apart as he came in.

"So Andret spoke truth," said the King.

"And what truth was that?" said Iseult, gathering up her hair.

"He told me that there was love between Tristan and you; and I would not believe. I told him that I would not believe until I saw the thing with my own eyes. —I trusted you both."

"Trust us still," said Iseult. "I do love Tristan, why should I not? He is your kinsman, and mine. I nursed him when he was sick enough to die, and he is become like a brother to me. And in the way that I love him, so he loves me."

"I wish that I could believe you," said the King. "I would give all that I possess to be able to believe you." And to Tristan he said, "She shall be to me as she was before, as though nothing of this had happened. But you must leave my Court." And he spoke gently, but his hand was on his sword.

And Tristan went, he and Gorvenal, and took lodgings with an old swordsmith in the town inland of the castle.

"It would be better that we go far away from here," said Gorvenal. "Let us go and seek adventure else-where."

"More dragons to kill?" said Tristan, and he laughed, with his head in his hands. "Dear, sensible Gorvenal, it would be best that we go to the farthest ends of the earth. But I can no more leave the Queen than I can pluck the living heart out of my breast."

Now it was coming on to high summer, and at that time of year, when there was peace in the land, the King and his Court would leave the grim castle on its headland, and spread out into the wooden Halls and bowers among the gardens and the little hardy apple orchards on the landward side. And the Queen had lodgings of her own close beside a little stream that flowed out of the woods and went purling down to the cove below the castle, so that it was always cool on the hottest August days.

And the Queen sent Brangian by night with a message, to Tristan's lodging, bidding him find means to meet her, if he would not have her die of longing to be with him again. And Tristan sent back word: "Keep a watch at twilight on the stream that flows past your bower, and if a branch comes floating by, keep watch still; and if a piece of bark carved with a five-pointed star comes floating after, then I shall be waiting under the wild peartree where the stream comes out of the woods, and it will be safe for you to come to me."

So every twilight, Iseult or Brangian watched the

stream, until one evening the branch followed by the five-pointed star came floating down, and then the Queen slipped out and away in the dusk, to find Tristan waiting for her under the wild peartree. And after this happened the first time, it happened many times again.

And then Andret, and the Lords who followed him, began to wonder whether Tristan and the Queen had parted indeed, or whether they had found means to meet in secret. And Andret went to a certain dwarf about the Court, a man who he had befriended from time to time; a man who possessed ancient skills and could read the answers to all questions in the stars, and bade him find out whether or no the Queen and Tristan were still lovers. So the dwarf looked into the stars all one long night, and said, "The Queen and the Lord Tristan are still meeting in secret, and if the King comes with me, he shall see them for himself."

And Andret took the dwarf to the King. "Give out that you are going on a hunting trip, but turn back. This night, thinking you safe away, they will meet under the big wild peartree where the stream comes out of the woods."

"Is this the truth?" said the King.

"Come with me and see," said the dwarf, "and if I lie, you have my full leave to cut off my head."

"If you lie, I shall not ask your leave," said the King.

So the King called for his horses and hounds and rode out as though for hunting, giving it out that he would be gone seven days. But before he was half a day's ride from Tintagel, he made an excuse to leave the rest of the hunting party to go on without him, and turned back to where the dwarf was waiting. Together they went to where the wild peartree grew on the edge of the woods, and the King helped the dwarf up into it and then climbed up after him.

Dusk came, and a moon rose over the hills, casting its snail-shine of silver across the sky. And with the moon, Tristan came up the stream side. He broke off a branch from the peartree and sent it down the stream, then pulled a piece of bark from one of the ancient silver birches close by, and sat down on the bank to scratch with his dagger the five-pointed star that would call Iseult out to him, and sent it after the branch. And all the while the King and the dwarf watched him through the branches overhead.

Now just below the tree, where Tristan sat, the stream broadened into a little pool and the water was quiet under the bank; and as the moon rose higher it turned the surface of the water to a trembling mirror, so that Tristan, leaning forward, could see his own head and shoulders reflected in it, and the dark branches of the peartree beyond—and clear against the moonlight, the outline of two figures among the branches!

Then Tristan knew that Andret or maybe even the King himself, or both of them, were watching him, watching for Iseult. And there was nothing he could do;

the branch and the star had long since gone on their way, and Iseult would be coming swiftly in answer. He had no means of warning her, and if he went away she would come, and finding no one there, might betray herself to the watchers in the tree. Even if he went to meet her and turn her back, they had seen him send the message, and would guess the meaning of what they saw. There was nothing to be done but wait for her to come, and try to warn her under their watchful gaze. And if he failed, it would be death for them both, he knew that; and for himself, he was past caring overmuch; but for her. . . .

He gave no sign of what he had seen, but sat quietly waiting. And as he waited he heard once or twice a faint rustle that was not the wind in the branches overhead.

Iseult received his message, and as usual slipped away with Brangian's help and hurried gladly to meet her love. But when she came near to the tree, and saw Tristan sitting on the bank, he never moved, and this seemed strange to her, for usually at first sight of her coming, he would leap up and come striding to catch her in his arms. And so she walked more slowly herself. And as she drew nearer still, he made a tiny gesture of warning towards the tree behind him. And glancing up, she saw the shadows of the two watchers in the branches. And she understood.

So she said, cool and clear, "My Lord Tristan, why did you send for me?"

"I must speak with you alone," said Tristan, "for I sorely need your help."

"My help? In what way would that be?"

"To soften the King's unjust anger towards me, that I may return to Court, for it is an ill thing to be ordered from his presence like a disobedient hound; and all men talk against me."

"They talk against both of us," said Iseult, "and the fault is yours, for you should have remembered that we are not indeed brother and sister, and that therefore we cannot be together freely as brother and sister would be, without setting dark suspicions in people's minds."

"If I should have remembered, should not you?" demanded Tristan.

"I should indeed, but you are a man and wiser than I, and so you must bear the chief blame."

"I will bear it gladly, if you help me, Iseult; would you not help your brother?"

"Not if he had brought the anger of my Lord upon me," said Iseult; and all the while, she was aware to her fingertips of the listeners overhead in the pear-tree, and she made a sob come into her voice—which indeed was not hard. "I have been sick at heart through your fault, for I cannot be happy while my Lord looks at me coldly and with doubt in his eyes. Now, if you ever felt a brother's fondness for me, go away, and leave me to win back my Lord's love as best I may."

And Tristan bent his head as though in defeat. "If you will not help me, then you will not, and I will never be asking you anything again. Go home now, and a good night to you, Iseult."

And Iseult turned and walked away down the stream side; while Tristan stood and watched her go, and heard again the faint rustling in the tree above him, that was not the wind. And then he turned and walked away also, with his head on his breast. There was a sickness in his belly and a foul taste in his mouth, and he hated Iseult in that moment, almost as much as he hated himself.

Then among the branches of the peartree King Marc drew his dagger and turned upon the dwarf beside him. But the dwarf saw the silver flash of the blade in the moonlight, and dropped from the branch and ran, doubling and twisting like a hare, and was away into the woods before the King could catch him.

And the stream ran on, quietly under the moon.

Next morning, King Marc went to the Queen in her bower, and told her how he had been hiding in the tree, and had heard all that passed between her and Tristan the night before, and begged her to forgive him, and make peace again between him and Tristan.

But Iseult knew that she must not seem too eager. "Truly I am thankful that the shadow between us is past," she said. "But it was through Tristan that your anger first fell upon me, and if you bring him back to

Court, can I be sure that the thing will not happen
again?"

"Sweet," said the King, "I have begged your for-
giveness for doubting you; be generous to both of us,
and I will never doubt you or him again."

So Tristan returned to Court. And for a while, all
was as it had been in the early days between himself
and King Marc and Iseult the Queen.

NINE

THE LEPER'S CLOAK

AGAIN the summer turned to autumn, and the
winter passed, and the gorse flamed along the headlands. And the love between Tristan and Iseult would
not let them be, dragging at them as the moon draws
the tides to follow after it, until at last, whether they
would or no, they came together again.

And all the while, Andret watched.

One night on the edge of summer, the Queen went
early to her bower, saying that her head ached for
there was thunder in the air, and she would be alone.
And soon after, Andret saw that Tristan's place in the
King's Hall was empty, and he, too, rose and slipped
out, following the champion of Cornwall.

He knew that it would be useless to go himself to
the King, for Marc would not believe any word he
said, but there were others about the Court who would
carry a message for a gold piece slipped into the hand;
and so later still, one of the castle servants came to the

King with word that the Queen begged him to go to
to her instantly in her bower.

And when he came striding into the bower, brushing aside Brangian, who tried to hold him back, he
saw two heads on the embroidered pillow, one red, and
one dark.

Then the King's wrath was terrible, all the more
terrible because of the love he had for his Queen and
his kinsman, and he waited to hear no more excuses,
but shouted up the guard. They came bursting in as
Tristan, still half-asleep, sprang from the bed and
reached for his sword. He fought like a wild boar at
bay, but he was one blade against many, and he was
beaten back to the wall, and made captive and dragged
away. And all the while Iseult crouched beside the
hearth, as still as though she had been turned to stone.
And the King never once looked her way. Only when
all was over, and she rushed to the door, she found her
way barred by crossed spears.

Next day, Tristan and Iseult were brought before
a Council of the Chiefs and the Churchmen and the
Lawmakers of Cornwall, to be tried for their betrayal
of the King. They made no defence, for they would no
longer make their love for each other seem smaller
and less worthy by denying it. And they were found
guilty and condemned to die; Iseult by fire, which by
the law of the land was the proper punishment for a
Queen who had betrayed her Lord; Tristan by being
broken over a great wheel.

In the time before the day appointed for their deaths, only one of the King's Lords dared to speak to Marc at all, let alone plead for mercy for them; and that one was Dynas the High Steward.

"This is surely a cruel thing that you do," said Dynas, and knew that he took his own life in his hands by saying it. "And the cruelty is against yourself as well as the Queen and the Lord Tristan; for in slaying them, I know well enough that you slay the two who are dearest to you on earth."

"You were never a man to care much for danger," said the King, "but you were never in greater danger than you are now." And he spoke between shut teeth, like a man speaking through the pain of a spear wound.

"I do not think so," said Dynas. "For you are a just man, and to slay me for speaking the truth would be unjust—even more unjust than to slay those two. My Lord King, neither man nor woman can choose who their love goes out to; and death is too great a price to demand, and cannot bring love back to you. Banish Tristan from Cornwall—I will take it upon my own honour to see that he does not return—and take the Queen once more into your life; use her gently, and it may be that she will turn to you yet."

"No," said the King, *"I will make an end."*

By dawn on the appointed day, all the preparations had been made. People had been summoned from far and wide to witness the deaths of Tristan and the Queen. And great was the grief, and loud the wailing of the women; for Tristan was dear to all the ordinary folk of Cornwall, their champion and their hope; and Iseult had made herself beloved in her husband's Kingdom as she had been in her father's.

Tristan was to die in the morning, and Iseult after noon; and so he was led out first by the men of the King's bodyguard. Now the chosen place of execution was some distance from the castle; and on the way to it they passed a little chapel, set high on the very lip of the cliffs above the sea; and when they came close to it, Tristan said to the Captain of the Guard, "The sun is scarce yet clear of the hills, and we have time to spare on this walk that we are taking. And indeed you thrust me forth this morning so early that I have had no time to make my peace with God, as I have sore need to be making it. Therefore give me leave to go in yonder and pray."

The Captain of the Guard considered a moment, and then he shrugged. "There's no harm, that I can see. But I and another of us will come in with you."

"What I have to say is for God's ear, not for yours," said Tristan. And then, as the man hesitated, he added, half-smiling, "Are you afraid that I shall escape you? I know that chapel as well as you do. There is but one narrow door to it, and one small high window above a sheer drop to the sea. I'd as soon be broken on the wheel as on the black rocks down yonder."

And they knew that it was true as to the door and the window, and so they let him go into the little chapel alone and close the door behind him. "It is but common charity to allow him—and he about to die," they said among themselves.

But as soon as the door was shut behind him, Tristan shot the bolt, taking care to make no sound that could be heard from outside. Then he crossed to the window that showed a tiny square of blank blue above the altar. He reached up and caught the sill and pulled himself up to it. He got his head and shoulders through, then a knee. Below him, far, far below, a sea as blue as a kingfisher's mantle creamed upon fanged black rocks; and a gull skimmed the chapel wall, almost brushing his face with its wings. He thrust himself further out, reached for a stone that gave a handhold above the window, and drew the other leg under him. The gulls wove their white curves of flight across the face of the cliffs below him; the jump would have been death to any other man, but Tristan had learned well from his masters in his Lothian boyhood, and had not forgotten how to make the Hero Leap. He filled himself with air until he felt as light as the wheeling seabirds, and drew himself together and sprang out and down.

He took the sea like a down-flung javelin, and the water closed over his head; but he leapt up again into the light, and the next wave gathered him and flung him shoreward. He clung to a rock, and between wave and wave, pulled himself ashore. And keeping close in under the cliffs, he made his way along to a place where he could regain the cliff top well out of sight from the chapel and the King's warriors watching at its door. Then he set off back towards Tintagel.

He had not gone far when rounding a bend in the track where it circled a tump of wind-shaped hawthorns, he came face to face with Gorvenal!

They made no outcry of greeting; but Gorvenal stood stock still and the colour drained from his face till he was white to the lips. And seeing his look, Tristan said, "Och no! It is I, not my seadripping ghost—it was to be the wheel, not drowning for me, remember."

But even as he spoke, Gorvenal flung his arms round him, and hugged him fiercely close, then held him off at arms' length to look at him. "Swift now, is the hunt behind you?"

"Not yet," Tristan said. "I will tell you all the story later, there is no time now."

"There's not indeed," said Gorvenal, "for the sooner we are many miles from here, the better. See, here are your sword and your harp. I would not be spending one night more in Tintagel, and I would not be leaving them behind me." And from under his cloak he pulled out the embroidered harp-bag that he had slung across his shoulder, and Tristan's beloved sword with the notched blade.

Tristan took the sword from him and belted it on. "Was there ever a time when I could not count on Gorvenal in my need? I shall have need of this. Let you keep my harp for me, until maybe I have a need for that also."

And he set his hand an instant on Gorvenal's shoulder, and then walked on, the way that he had been going.

Gorvenal swung round and went after him. "Are you mad? This is the way back to Tintagel."

"I am knowing that well enough. Could I make my escape and leave Iseult to die in the flames? I must save her today, or die with her; there is no other way for me. —But the hazard is mine and none of yours. Go your way, brother, with my thanks for bringing me my sword."

"As to that, I have my own sword also, and two blades are better than one," said Gorvenal. "And if you are for Tintagel again, then so am I."

And they went on together.

Soon, coming to the edge of the woods, they looked out towards the fortress on its headland, and saw the place made ready for the Queen's execution, between the woodshore and the sea, with the pyre already built in the midst of it, and all about it, the great crowd of people who had gathered to see her die.

"And now what would you have us do?" asked Gorvenal, crouching behind a hawthorn bush.

"They have not yet brought her out; when they do, maybe God will help us to know the thing that must be done. Meanwhile there is nothing we can do but wait."

And as they waited, just as the far-off gates of Tintagel opened, and the King himself, amidst the rest of
his bodyguard, came down between the timber halls
and the apple orchards toward the execution place,
another band of men came down the track from the
woods behind Tristan and Gorvenal. A little band, a
terrible band, wearing the long hooded cloaks and
carrying the wooden warning clappers that marked
them for lepers, who counted as already dead.

Gorvenal drew further from the track, as all men
did when such a company came by, and Tristan made
to do the same; then checked, and stepped forward
directly into their path.

"Where are you away to, friends?"

The lepers checked, for they were not used to being
spoken to by living men, then one who seemed to be
the leader among them said in a cracked and husky
voice, "To Tintagel as all Cornwall goes today, though
with heavy hearts, to see them burn the Queen."

"Then you would save the Queen if you could?"
said Tristan.

"If it were worth our while."

"Lend me your cloak and clapper, and there will be
no burning in Tintagel today," Tristan said. And to
Gorvenal, "Have you any money? It's a gold piece I
am needing for this man and his comrades."

"You are mad!" said Gorvenal.

"Maybe; that is the second time today that you have
told me so. But I need the gold piece."

And while the others looked on, he took the coin his friend brought from the breast of his tunic, and dropped it into the bandaged hand that the leper held out for it.

"It's many a long year since any man would wear my cloak of his own free will," the man said. And he pulled off his stinking rags; and Tristan took them, scarcely even shuddering for there was no time, and flung on the cloak, pulling the hood forward over his face.

"Here is my cloak; it is wet from the sea, but it will serve to cover your sores. Bide here in hiding, while I go on with your companions."

"I also," said Gorvenal.

But Tristan shook his head. "Bide you here. If all goes well, one of us will be enough for the task; if aught goes ill, then I may need you, still free, to get the Queen away."

So Tristan went on with the lepers, swinging his wooden clapper, and with their dreadful cry in his ears: "Unclean! Unclean!"

When they reached the execution place, the Queen, clad in nothing but a white shift, and her wonderful red hair falling loose about her, was already being bound to the stake, while men waited with lighted torches, and the King stood by with a frozen face to see it done.

"Come," said Tristan, to the rest of the grey band behind him; and they made towards the King. No man sought to bar their passage, and so they came to him up a clear road, the people falling back on either side like barley when a reaping-hook cuts its swath. And Tristan knelt before the King, keeping his hands that had no sores on them hidden in his sleeves, and his face that was not eaten away hidden in the shadows of his hood.

"Oh Lord King! A boon!" he cried, making his voice cracked and hoarse.

And, "A boon! A boon!" cried the lepers crowding behind him.

The King looked at them with stone eyes in a stone face. "You choose a strange moment to come asking a boon."

"Not so strange," said Tristan, "for the boon we ask is this, that you give us the Queen, to be of our company."

A gasp ran through the crowd, but King Marc never moved. "*Give you the Queen?*" he said; and his voice was stony as all else about him.

"If she is to die a shameful death, we can offer her one more shameful than the fire. —Slower than the fire, but maybe uglier."

And the lepers behind him clamoured, "Give her to us! Give! Give!"

And the King's stone face broke up into a sudden agony of rage, and he shouted to the executioners, "Cut the Queen loose, and give her to these creatures!"

Then Iseult began to scream and scream, and cling to the stake as though it were her only hope; and when

Tristan in his leper's guise, sprang up onto the piled faggots to seize her, she fought him like a wild thing; while the crowd set up a ragged shout of angry protest, though with the King's eye upon them and his nobles and his bodyguard all about, they dared no more. And then Iseult, thrusting the leper away with both hands, caught a glimpse of crimson silk at his breast and felt the skin clean and healthy under his foul cloak, and heard his whisper close to her ear, "Iseult! It is I! Do not betray me!"

She went on screaming, but many of those standing round saw that she ceased to fight, as though despair had come upon her, and allowed herself to be dragged down from the pyre and into the midst of the little knot of lepers, and away up the track towards the woods. And again the people parted to let them through.

TEN

THE SWORD AND
THE GLOVE

$\mathcal{M}$EANWHILE, the warriors waiting before the little clifftop chapel had long since grown impatient. "He is over-long at his prayers," they said. And at last when they had called and got no answer, they broke the door down—and found the place empty!

The Captain sprang for the window and peered down, thinking to see Tristan's broken body on the rocks below. But there were only the waves, and the seabirds wheeling by.

When word of Tristan's escape was brought to the King, his wrath was terrible, and he sent out his warriors to seek him out and bring him back, living or dead. But no sign of Tristan was to be found. They came up with the lepers, but the Queen was no longer with them, and they had a tale to tell of how a mighty and terrible warrior had sprung out upon them as they passed some bushes, and snatched her away from them. And under a hawthorn tree the searchers found

Tristan's sea-wet cloak lying where it had been tossed aside. But there was nothing that that could tell them.

And of Tristan and Iseult, they found no sign at all. They and Gorvenal had vanished into the wild as completely as so many rags of morning mist when the sun climbs high above the hills.

Only one living thing out of Tintagel knew the way that they were gone, and that was Bran, Tristan's favourite hound, who followed them by scent, and came up with them next day. And it was well for them that he did so, for they had need of a hunting dog in time to come.

They held eastward and eastward, away and away from Tintagel, pushing on all day and lying up in some thicket for a few hours each night. When Iseult grew faint with weariness and could walk no more, Tristan or Gorvenal carried her; and so they came at last to a little lost valley by which a stream threaded down from the high black moors where the stone circles of forgotten people stood against the sky. Hawthorn and alder and hazel shaded it over, and the small dark thick-set oak trees of the ancient forest reached up from below as though they held up their arms to receive it. And between the moors and the forest, the stream broadened into a little pool where the deer came to drink at dawn and sunset.

"Surely here we shall be safe," said Tristan. "We are full three days from Tintagel and it is many years since the King hunted these hills."

"The hunting will be good here," said Gorvenal, "and since we must turn hunter if we are to live . . ."

And Iseult said in a voice that was soft as the wood-pigeons among the trees, "This is such a place as our valley in Wales. We shall know happiness here—for a while."

So there Tristan and Gorvenal built a hut beside the stream; and there the three of them took up their lives. Iseult had no garment but her white shift, and so the men gave her their tunics, and went in their shirts until they could dress themselves in the rough-cured skins of the deer they shot for food. They made themselves bows of yew wood from the forest, the strings braided of the red hairs that Iseult plucked for them from her head; and when they needed food they took out Bran and went hunting, or set snares for small game, or fished in the stream for the rose-specked trout. And Iseult, with her knowledge of herbs, gathered from the high moors and the stream sides and the forest round about, all the plants that had leaves or roots or berries that were good to eat. And so they contrived to live well enough.

Above all, they were happy, Iseult missed nothing of being a Queen; and Tristan had his friend and his hound, his harp to make music, and Iseult beside him, and there was nothing more he hungered for, in all the world. And if Gorvenal regretted anything at all, there was no one but himself knew of it.

It was young summer when they came to the hidden

valley; and three times the hawthorn trees were rusted with berries and the hazelnuts fell into the stream. And three times winter came and they huddled about the fire in the smoky bothie and threw on logs from the wood-store outside, while Tristan woke the music of his harp and sang to them the haunting story-songs of Lothian and Cornwall and of Ireland too. Three times the hazel catkins shone yellow as pale sunshine against the dark of the moors, and three times the hawthorns were white-curdled with blossom and the blossom fell and the foxgloves stood tall along the wood-shore and the cuckoos called all day.

And then on the edge of another autumn, one evening Tristan and Iseult sat before the hut watching the stream run by and the twilight come creeping up from the trees. They were alone, for Gorvenal had taken Bran as he sometimes did, and gone off on a solitary hunting trip. And Iseult drew close to Tristan as though suddenly she were afraid, and said, "Do you feel anything?"

"A little shiver of wind," said Tristan.

"No, not that."

"A moth brushed by my cheek."

"No, not that."

"What is it then, Iseult?"

"A shadow. There is a shadow fallen over us."

"Heart-of-my-heart, it is only the twilight."

"No, it is not the twilight," said Iseult.

"Then it is the time of year, and the leaves falling."

"No, it is not that, for I have ever loved the winter, and the hut sheltering us like wings folded close between us and the cold."

And she got up and went into the hut, and when in a little he followed her, she was combing her hair by the light of a rush dip, as she had been combing it by the light of a fine wax taper when he had come to tell her that they were sailing for Cornwall on the morning tide.

Now that very day, far off in Tintagel, the King called for his hounds to ride hunting. In the long three years he had hunted the hills of Cornwall far and wide, he and his Court like the wild riders of Gwyn ap Nudd; for he had no more any pleasure in feasting or harpsong; and when the work of Kingship was done, there was nothing gave him any pleasure but to be out after the red deer or the black boar or the fanged and red-eyed wolf of the wilderness. So yet again, he ordered out his horses and his hounds for next day; but this time he said to his Chief Huntsman, "I am weary of the old hunting-runs, are there no hills in Cornwall where we have not hunted before?"

"There are the moors away westward toward Lyoness," said the Chief Huntsman. "It is many years since you hunted so far afield."

So the next day King Marc and his companions rode eastward toward the high moors of Lyoness. And three days later they set up their hunting camp. All next day they hunted; the hunting was good, and they killed three times; but when the hound-pack was counted at feeding time, that evening, one of them was missing. It was a good hound, and one of the King's favourites, and the Chief Huntsman at once called out some of his men and set off to find it.

Tristan and Iseult had heard no sound of that day's hunting; but at dusk as they sat once more before the hut doorway, Iseult said suddenly, "What sound is that?"

And Tristan listened, and said, "It sounds like a lost hound, but like enough it is a wolf."

And they listened together for a long time, but it did not come again. And presently they went into the hut and lay down on the bed-place, leaving the fire burning in the doorway as they had done often enough before when there were wolves about. And Tristan drew his sword from its sheath and laid it naked beside him.

All night long the King's Chief Huntsman searched for the lost hound, until at last, at the dark hour before dawn, he came to the edge of the trees and saw the white thread of a stream coming down from the high moors; and above him among the streamside hazels the gleam of a fire; and thinking that it might belong to some shepherds or charcoal burners, he dismounted and hitched his horse to a low-hanging branch, and turned upstream towards the red flicker, meaning to ask the people up there if they had seen any sign of a strayed hound.

So he came to the fire, his feet silent on the stream-side grass, and found that it burned before the door-way of a hut, and peering in, he saw by the dying fire-light a man and a woman asleep on the piled bracken of the bed-place. Their faces were in shadow, but the flame-light struck answering flame from the red of the woman's outflung hair; and the man's sword lying ready to his hand had a small piece broken out of the blade. No one knowing Tristan could mistake that notched blade.

The huntsman turned silently away and went back down the streamside to where he had left his horse; and mounted and rode back towards the King's camp, and before he had gone three bow-shots on his way, there was a yelping and a rustling in the undergrowth and the lost hound came bounding out to follow at his horse's heels.

The camp was still asleep when he reached it, and he roused Marc's armour-bearer from before the entrance of the King's bothie, and went in to him.

"Have you found Gelert?" said the King.

"Aye, but it was not for that I woke you. I found something else."

"And what is that, that because of it you must rouse me from my sleep?"

"A few miles from here," said the huntsman, and

suddenly he was afraid of what he had to tell, "there is a hut, and a fire burning before it, and inside a man and a woman sleeping on the bed-place."

The King came to his elbow. "What man? And what woman?"

"I could not see their faces," said the huntsman, "but the woman had red hair, and the man a piece broken out of his sword blade."

The King held silent a long moment. Then he said, "Bid my armour-bearer to fetch my horse and have it ready beyond the camp as soon as may be; for I would see this man and this woman."

So the King's horse was made ready, and he and the Chief Huntsman set out. It was just at daybreak when they reached the place where the stream came down from the high moors, and the last light of the dying fire still glimmered among the hazel trees. Then the King bade his huntsman wait with the horses. And he went on up the streamside, his own sword naked in his hand. He came to the entrance of the hut, and stood looking in. And he saw by the grey dawn light, Tristan and Iseult lying on the bed-place; and he knew that he had only to step over the threshold and use his sword, first on Tristan and then on the Queen, for they were completely at his mercy. And because they were so completely at his mercy, he could not do it. He stood there so long that the grey light began to be watered with gold, and soon he knew they must wake. And as he looked, it seemed to him that he had never seen

Iseult so beautiful, and his heart had never longed for her more. And when he looked at Tristan his old love for his kinsman knotted in his belly.

At last he unsheathed his sword, and stooping, took up Tristan's, and laid his own blade where it had been. And he stripped off one of his hunting gloves, and laid it lightly on Iseult's breast. For an instant she caught her breath and stirred in her sleep; then returned to her quiet breathing. And King Marc turned and went his way, sheathing the notched blade in place of his own.

ELEVEN

THE RING

WHEN Tristan and Iseult awoke, they found the King's sword lying in place of Tristan's, and the King's glove on the Queen's breast, and they knew that they were discovered.

"We must leave this place at once," Iseult said. "We dare not wait even for Gorvenal! Leave a sign for him, that he may follow the way we go: and we will strike further into the wilds."

"If we do that thing now that the King has found us and knows that we are together, it is in my heart that he will hunt us down," Tristan said. "We shall never hear a dog howling in the night without fearing the hunt on our trail. And yet—he found us here and could have slain us, and did not."

"What does it mean?" said Iseult.

Tristan shook his head. "I would not be knowing. I know only that he left us his message: the sword for me, and the glove for you." (And he remembered how on the day he brought Iseult from Ireland into Cornwall, King Marc had taken her hands in his and said that they were cold but his were large enough to warm them.) "The way back is clear—at least for you, Iseult."

"I would not be taking it, without you."

"There may be a way back for me, too, I do not know. I must put myself at the King's mercy; that is the meaning of the sword."

"I have been happy here, and there's no wish in me to be Queen of Cornwall again."

"Better to be Queen of Cornwall than listen for hounds baying on your trail for as long as life lasts."

And at that instant they heard a hound baying in the distance and Iseult shuddered and drew herself together with a gasp, and looked at Tristan through widened eyes.

"You see?" said Tristan, and put his arms round her and held her close. "Heart-of-my-heart, that is Bran. —Gorvenal is back from his hunting. —But, you see how it would be?"

When Gorvenal appeared, and flung down the buck that he had killed, while Bran came to lick Tristan's hand and then lay down panting and pleased with his hunting, Tristan told his friend the thing that had happened; and Gorvenal agreed that the time had come to be going back to Tintagel.

So they left the little bothie beside the stream, for the grass to grow fresh over the scars where the hearth fire had been, and went back to Tintagel and the King.

It was torchlighting time when they came to King Marc sitting in his High Seat with the stallion-carved foreposts; and he sat unmoving, his eyes upon them, as Tristan and Iseult walked up the empty Hall to stand before him.

The silence dragged out long and heavy as the stillness between lightning flash and thunder peal. And a dog at the King's feet whimpered, smelling grief and anger and love and hate hanging like the thunder in the air.

At last the King said, "So you read my message."

"We read your message," Tristan said, "and we came."

"That is well," said the King. "Listen now; I will take the Queen back into my Hall, into my heart. As for you, Tristan, who once I loved most dearly of all men in this world, I say to you only—'the world is wide.' "

Tristan looked straight and long into the King's eyes. "I had a hope that the way back was for me also, but it was only a small hope. The world is wide, as you say, my Lord the King."

"I give you until tomorrow's sun-up to gather what you would take with you and be gone from Tintagel. I give you three days to be out of Cornwall. You will never come back!"

Tristan bowed his head, then raised it and looked once more straight at the King. "In three days I will be gone from Cornwall. But if ever harm or sorrow come to Iseult at your hands, I shall hear of it, *and I shall come back!*"

Then Iseult spoke for the first time. "My Lord the King, if I am to be with you and be your wife again, I must end what has been between my Lord Tristan and me, not leave it hanging like a torn sleeve. Let you grant us a little time alone, to take our leave of each other."

The King pointed to a log on the fire already crumbling to white ash. "You have until that log burns through." And he rose and went to the inner doorway. But they knew that from the chamber beyond, he would hear when the log burned through and fell.

When they were alone, they moved close together; but they had no goodbyes to say, for they had said them all so many times that they were empty. And Tristan said only, speaking at half breath, "I leave Bran with you. Love him for my sake."

And Iseult said, "He shall be dearer to me than anything else in Cornwall, because he is your gift. And for you also I have a gift," and she pulled from her finger a heavy gold ring formed of curiously twined and twisted serpents, that had come with her from Ireland. "If ever you are in sore enough need of me, send me this back, and I will come to you though you send from the other end of the world. But be careful how you send it, for if you do, then I will come, though it be the death of both of us."

And Tristan took the ring and kissed it, and stowed it in the breast of his outworn shirt.

"One thing more," Iseult said. "Make me this promise, that all your life, if anything is asked of you in my name, you will do it. No matter how strange, or difficult, or perilous, or great, or small, if it be asked of you in the name of Iseult of Cornwall."

And this she asked, so that she might know in her heart thereafter, that she still held power over him, and power to call him back, even though she never used it to her dying day.

And Tristan knew why she asked, and he promised. "It shall be as you ask."

Iseult set her hands on either side of his face and drew him close and looked into his eyes. "I do not ask. I set you under Geis, according to the custom of my own people, for remember, Iseult of Cornwall is an Irishwoman still. And remember also that if you break your Geis you break your own honour with it, and your own life, and maybe all that is left of mine as well."

The burned log collapsed with slipping and rustling and a last shower of sparks, into the red heart of the fire.

Tristan went back to his old lodging, and gathered his own clothes and few belongings that were still there, and put on his fine mail shirt, while Gorvenal brought horses from the stable. And at dawn he rode out from Tintagel and headed eastward into the sunrise, with Gorvenal riding at his side. He never saw King Marc again, save once when King Marc did not know of it, but the King's sword was still in his scabbard, and his own notched blade in the King's.

TWELVE

WAR IN BRITTANY

TRISTAN and Gorvenal wandered up and down Britain and through other lands; and many the adventures they had, until at last they came to Brittany, and a part of Brittany that had once been fair but was now a wilderness. For three days they rode through it, and saw halls and strongholds and the traces of fields; but the halls were roofless and their hearths cold, and the fields lost under docks and brambles. And in all the land nothing moved but the creatures of the wild.

But on the third evening they came to a little chapel on a hill, and a hermit's cell beside it; and from the hermit's cell came the first gleam of firelight they had seen since they entered that land. So they rode towards it, and the old bent hermit came to the door, and asked, "What would you have of me, my sons?"

"A night's shelter," Tristan said. "A place by your fire, Old Father, since it seems there is no other warm hearth in all this land."

So that evening they sat by the hermit's fire, though they would take nothing from his meagre store of food, but ate what little they had in their own saddlebags. And when they had eaten, Tristan asked the meaning of the desolation all about them.

"Well may you ask," said the hermit, "for this land used to be as rich as any in the world, until sorrow came upon it. . . . You must know, then, that our King, Hoel, has a most beautiful daughter, and she was sought in marriage by one of his vassal lords, Duke Jovelin of Nantes. The King refused him—some say he was too proud to give his daughter to a vassal; some say she was unwilling. Then Jovelin thought to take her by force, and he roused out many of the other nobles to join him against the King. They have laid waste the land as you see, they have broken down all the royal castles, except Carhaix; and there, in his last remaining stronghold, the King is even now besieged, with his son Karherdin and a few chiefs who remain true to him."

"And where is this castle of Carhaix?" asked Tristan.

"Scarce two miles from here."

"Then if you will let us sleep by your fire tonight, it will be an easy ride in the morning."

"Dragons," said Gorvenal, "always there must be more dragons for you. Let you remember what came of the last time."

"I am remembering, and I am remembering," said Tristan, gentling his sword hilt.

Next morning they took their leave of the hermit, and set out for Carhaix. They found Duke Jovelin's warhost encamped round about, but seeing that they were but two horsemen, no one thought it worth while to turn them back, and so they came beneath the timber walls of the castle. The King himself—Tristan knew it must be the King by the golden crest on his helmet—stood on the ramparts, looking out over the rebel warhost, and Tristan brought his horse close and called up to him, "My Lord the King, have you use for two more swords?"

The King looked down at him and laughed, like an old dog-fox barking. "We have no use for two more mouths; supplies are short enough as it is. It was a valiant offer, strangers, but this is not your quarrel, take my thanks with you and ride away."

"As to the mouths, my sword-brother and I have seen lean times before now, and we're knowing well enough how to take a knot in our bellies. I am in need of a good quarrel—may I not have a share in yours?"

And a tall ugly young man with sandy hair and a big nose and a laughing mouth, who stood close beside the King, said quickly, "Two good swords are worth half a loaf a day, my father; and if this bold stranger wants a share in our quarrel—well, it's big enough, there's no need to play the miser with it!"

So in the end the timber gates were swung back just wide enough to let horse and rider through, while the warriors stood ready against a rush by Jovelin's men.

And the first hand that came out to greet Tristan as he clattered over the gate-sill with Gorvenal still behind him, was the big bony hand of the Prince Karherdin.

But Tristan and Gorvenal were not the only riders to draw rein before the great gates of Carhaix that day, for a while after noon, a herald rode out from the rebel warhost, to bring a challenge from Duke Jovelin to any man in the castle who would come out to meet him in single combat.

When he had received the message, the King said, "If I were but twenty years—but ten years—younger and quicker . . . !"

And the Prince Karherdin shrugged and said, "If I could do any good by taking up the challenge, I'd not hang back. But I know Jovelin's fighting strength; there's not a man in the Kingdom to stand a moth's chance in a candleflame, in single combat with that one."

And the rest of the warriors looked at each other and away again. And some half reached for their swords; but no one offered to take up the challenge.

Then Tristan, who had waited for the others, feeling that they had first right, said, "My Lord the King, I have been but a few hours among you, but give me leave, none the less, to meet this Duke Jovelin. I have answered a like challenge before, against worse odds, and that time I had the victory."

So the herald went back from Carhaix with word

that Tristan of Lothian (for he could no more be calling himself Tristan of Cornwall) would take up the
challenge of Duke Jovelin, and come out to meet him
an hour before sunset. And at the appointed time, the
great gates opened again, and Tristan walked out, with
his sword naked in his hand. And in the clear space
below the walls, Duke Jovelin strode out to meet him.
The westering sun jinked on their weapons, and their
shadows streamed out from them sideways like the
shadows of giants on the grass. And from the ramparts
of Carhaix and ranks of the rebel warhost, besiegers
and defenders looked on.

Then the heralds cried out the challenge and ac-
ceptance, and the fight began. It was a long and bitter
struggle, slow and wary at first as when hounds circle
each other seeking for an opening; both champions
striving for position with the sun behind them and
dazzling into the other's eyes, then growing swifter and
more fierce as they closed in and the blades began to
ring together and the sparks to fly from their blows.
Once, Jovelin took a gash in the thigh, and once
Tristan took a thrust in the shoulder; but for a long
while neither could gain an advantage over the other.
And then at last, as Tristan stepped back from a savage
flurry of strokes, Jovelin, pressing after, missed his
thrust and Tristan had their blades locked together;
for an instant they battled, eye to eye and hilt to hilt,
and then the Duke's sword, wrenched from his grasp,

spun a shining arc through the air to land, point down, far over toward the rebel camp. And Duke Jovelin stood defenceless with Tristan's blade at his throat.

Then the rebel warriors set up a shout and broke forward to their leader's aid; but Jovelin shouted to them where he stood, "Back, dogs! Back, I say! I'll not have my honour blackened for me by my friends!" And they checked and drew back to their watching line. And to Tristan he said, "Tristan of Lothian, it seems that I must yield to you for life or death."

Tristan lowered his sword. "These are my terms: that you shall bid your men to bring out from your camp enough food to provision Carhaix for one week, or you shall lie in the castle dungeons and we'll fight on hungry as we are. The choice is yours, my Lord Jovelin."

Then Duke Jovelin smiled, and they looked at each other not as enemies but simply as two fighting men. And he said, "I've no liking for dungeons. I choose to provision Carhaix for a week."

"That is a wise choice, and I for one am glad of it," said Tristan. "I'm thinking it would be a fine and pleasant thing that the first of the supplies arrives in time for supper."

Then Duke Jovelin called out certain of his men and gave them their orders; and by the last light of the sunset and then by the flare of torches, the bags of flour and the barrels of salt meat were brought, and received

by the warriors at the castle gates, while Duke Jovelin
stood by as Tristan's prisoner to see it done. And when
the last sack and barrel had been carried inside Carhaix, the two champions parted, and the Duke went to
where his sword still stood upright in the ground, and
plucked it out and walked back to his own camp fires,
while Tristan, with the sleeve of his tunic oozing red
under his mail, went back into Carhaix.

Again the first to greet him was Karherdin. "I should
hate you," said Karherdin.

"But you do not," said Tristan.

"I do not," said the Prince; and he put his arm
round Tristan's shoulders. "We shall sup tonight. But
before we do, you must have that wound seen to. Come
to the women's quarters, and my sister will tend it for
you."

So Tristan went with Karherdin to the women's
quarters, behind the Great Hall of the stronghold. A
maiden stood beside the fire, drawing a silver bell on a
green thread along the floor for a kitten to play with.
She had brown hair that fell forward on either side of
her face, so that he could not see at first what like she
was. But he saw her hands against the crimson stuff of
her gown, and they were white and almost transparent
as the point-petalled windflowers of the woods.

Karherdin said, "Here is our champion, who has
won us another week of eating. He has not come
scatheless out of the fight, and I have brought him to

you to tend his wound." And as she looked up and
smiled, he said to Tristan, "This is my sister, the
Princess Iseult."

And that was how Tristan first saw Iseult of the
White Hands.

The day after, a messenger got into the castle in secret,
bringing word for King Hoel that two of his nephews
were hurrying to his aid, with two hundred fighting
men, and food to supply the castle for many weeks.
Then the old King sent for Tristan and Karherdin and
told them the good news. "They can scarcely be here
before noon tomorrow," he said. "But from early morning we shall keep a watch; and when they appear, we
must sally out to cover them from Jovelin's warhost
and bring them safe into the castle. I shall remain here
with twenty men to hold the gate; the command of the
rest I give to the both of you together."

Next day a short while after noon, King Hoel's kins-
men were sighted, and the gates were opened and the
sally party marched out, Tristan and Karherdin at
their head, shoulder to shoulder under the blue and
emerald standard of Carhaix.

They had meant only to cover the two hundred safe
into the castle; but Duke Jovelin's men, on their lower
ground, could not see the dust-cloud of the relief force;
and seeing only the band that came out through the
castle gate, they set up a great shout and sped roaring
to the attack. Then King Hoel's nephews heard the

sounds of fighting from afar, and came charging over the hill to take the rebel warhost in the rear. And all at once there was full battle raging across the level ground before the walls of Carhaix.

Long and savagely they fought, the fortunes of the battle swinging now this way and now that; and at one time Karherdin, cut off from his companions, was surrounded by Duke Jovelin's men, and in sore danger of being cut down or taken captive. But Tristan, seeing his desperate peril, charged to his rescue with a band of his own men behind him, and broke through the enemy ranks to the Prince's side.

Then they turned together upon the enemy, and made a new charge; and this new charge, fierce and stronger than any that had gone before, broke the battle-mass of Duke Jovelin's fighting men and swept them from the field.

Before sunset, forty of the rebel chiefs and their men with them were captives, and many more were dead. And Duke Jovelin himself, forced to submit, had sworn on the hilt of his sword to be King Hoel's loyal man from that day forth, and to restore to him all that he had torn from him by war.

That night as they sat at meat in the Great Hall of Carhaix, and the Princess and her maidens went among the warriors keeping the wine cup filled, the old King turned to Tristan sitting beside him, and said, "Today it was as though I had two sons in battle below our walls. Two nephews, and two sons. And now it is in my mind, if you will have it so, to take you for another son indeed." And for a moment Tristan was not sure of his meaning. "The land has been laid waste because I would not give my daughter to a husband I deemed unworthy. Now the land will grow green again and fires will burn on the hearthstones, and for your part in this, I give her to you, for you are worthy of her."

And Tristan saw the Princess Iseult standing before him with a great wine cup in her hands; and this time her face was not hidden by her hair for the thick brown braids were bound back under goldwork for a festival; and he saw the colour flood into her cheeks, deep as the foxgloves of the Cornish woods, and her eyes bright and soft; and he knew that her heart was towards him.

And he thought, "Surely this is a thing that Fate has written on my forehead. My own Iseult is lost to me, and I shall never see her again. Now, here is another Iseult. If I refuse her, she will be shamed, and if I take her, there may be something of happiness for us both, even though it be a happiness with its wings clipped so that it cannot fly." So he said, "If the Princess will have it so, then I will have it so, and gladly."

And he set his hands over hers on the great wine cup, and bent his head, and drank.

THIRTEEN
THE HUNTING PARTY

 So Tristan and Iseult White-hands were married, and for a whole year they lived their lives together. But Tristan never grew to feel for her as a man should feel for his woman; as he would have felt if it had been the other Iseult beside him. He was always kind to her, but there was no fire nor joy nor laughter in the kindness, for all the fire and joy and laughter that had once been in him, he had left in Cornwall. Iseult White-hands never complained, never told anyone if she was unhappy, for she was always good at keeping secrets, much better than Iseult of Cornwall had ever been. But Karherdin her brother, who loved her dearly, saw how things were between her and Tristan, and determined to speak with him.

He watched his chance; and one day, riding on the seashore, he saw how Tristan let the reins fall slack on his horse's neck, and how he rode half-turned in the saddle and looking out to sea, quite forgetful of his companion. And he said, "What is it you see out there?"

Tristan started, and came back into himself. "Only the waves and the seabirds."

"Are you sure?" said Karherdin.

"What else should I see?"

"Cornwall lies that way." (For Tristan had long since told him he was from Cornwall after Lothian.)

"And why should I be looking towards Cornwall?"

"I was wondering if you were looking for the thing, whatever—*whoever*—it may be, that holds you from loving my sister as a man should love his wife."

Tristan started, and his hand on the rein set his horse dancing; and when he had quietened it, he turned to Karherdin and asked, "What makes you think that I do not?"

"I have watched you together often enough. And always—more and more of late—you are like a man whose heart is somewhere else, and his breast empty within him."

Tristan rode in silence a while, along the line between the wet sand and the dry; and then he said, "It is true as you say. I have no power to love your sister Iseult, for all the love that I have I left behind me long ago in Cornwall, with another Iseult."

"I have heard that the Queen of Cornwall bears that name," said Karherdin.

And again they rode in silence between the wet sand

and the dry. Then Karherdin said, "Men say that she is very fair."

"Men speak true," said Tristan. "She is more beautiful than any other woman that I have ever seen. But if she were bent and ugly as old Ginna who begs at the castle gate, still I must love her. . . . Day and night the longing for her drags at me. Day by day and night by night it grows worse and not easier. . . ." And again he set his horse dancing in protest. "Karherdin my brother, it is come to this—that I must go back and see her once more, or I think that I shall die or run mad!"

"And when you have seen her?"

"I do not know," Tristan said, and his voice was hoarse and weary as the voice of one who had lain too long wakeful and in pain. "It may be that by seeing her, I shall ease my heart and come back to Iseult White-hands. I know only that as I am I am no good to any woman, nor any man. But how should you understand?"

"Better, maybe, than you would think," said Karherdin, looking straight between his horse's ears. "For I too see a woman's face always between me and the sun."

And after a while, Tristan said, "Tell me, then?"

"It was before ever Duke Jovelin came seeking my sister's hand. One day when I was riding, I came upon a band of maidens gathering hawthorn branches, for it

was the first day of May. One of them—she seemed to
me the fairest of them all—told me her name was
Gargeolain, and we met again and again and made
secret promises to marry when she had seen another
summer go by, for she was very young. But I was called
away to trouble on my father's borders, and when I returned, they had forced her into marriage with a vassal
chief called Bedenis. —He was among those who besieged Carhaix last year."

"But if she was unwilling, why did she not tell them
she was yours? —Call on your father for aid?"

"She knew only that I was a man called Karherdin
—and that's no uncommon name in Brittany. I never
told her I was my father's son, for it was sweet to me to
be loved as a man and not a Prince. Oh, I had meant to
tell her later, but when I was sent away there was no
time; and so when Bedenis came seeking her, she could
say only, 'I am promised to a man called Karherdin'—
and he was not to be found."

"And you have never seen her since?"

"Yes, twice. Her Lord rides hunting almost every
day and never takes her with him, but keeps her close
shut in his stronghold, behind high walls, for he is a
most jealous man. And twice, passing by along the
track that leads below the castle mound, I have looked
up and seen her standing on the ramparts. A long way
off, but I could not be mistaken."

Then again they rode in silence between the dry
sand and the wet, until at last Tristan burst out, "Kar-

herdin my brother, for the sake of all that you feel for Gargeolain, help me to leave Brittany for Cornwall once more. I swear that I will come back."

And Karherdin said, "Now that the realm is at peace and we can be spared, let us go on a journey together. I hear that King Marc breeds fine horses, and I am minded to add to my stables. —It will serve as excuse at my father's Court."

So with only Gorvenal and a trusted armour-bearer of Karherdin's for company, they took ship and sailed for Cornwall, and made their way to the Hall of Tristan's old friend Dynas of Lidan, the High Steward. And Tristan begged him, "Go to the Queen for me, show her this ring and bid her to arrange two days' hunting in the White Lands. Bid her to see that they take the valley track, and at a certain point, I will be lying hidden among the bushes, and I will flick a green reed into her horse's mane, for a sign to her that I am there. —It is an old, idle trick of mine, she will remember. —And where she receives the sign, there let her persuade the King to halt and make his hunting camp for the night."

"Once," said Dynas, "I begged the King for your banishment in place of your death, and offered to pledge my own honour you should not return to Cornwall. The King would not listen to me, and therefore I hold myself free in this matter."

And he went to Tintagel, and contriving to get word

with the Queen alone, showed her the ring and gave
her Tristan's message.

She turned from white to red and back to white
again; but she made no sound and gave no sign, for
though they had drawn aside into an inner doorway,
they were in the same room in which the King and one
of his Lords were playing chess beside the hearth. Only
she turned to the chess-players. "My Lord, your High
Steward brings word of a fine twelve-point stag that
has been seen in the White Lands. Shall we go hunting
tomorrow? For truly I grow weary of Tintagel walls,
this fine blue autumn weather."

The High Steward returned with his message. And
when the shadows lengthened on the next evening,
Tristan and Karherdin were lying up in the heart of
a hawthorn thicket where the valley track led into the
White Lands. —It was from the thorns that fleeced all
the country round about with a snow of blossom in the
spring, that those hunting-runs got their name. They
had sent Gorvenal and Karherdin's armour-bearer back
with the horses to the High Steward's Hall, and they
were alone in the woods touched with the first fires of
autumn.

The shadows lengthened and lengthened and the
sunlight grew thick like floating gold-dust in the air.
And then at last they heard the sound of hooves and
feet far off down the track. Nearer and nearer came the
sounds, until the foremost of the hunting party came
into view; the servants, leading mules laden with

rolled-up tents and awnings, with pots and pans and great baskets of provisions and all the wherewithal to make the hunting camp. After they had gone by, came the stewards and cupbearers; and then the falconers with the hooded falcons on their fists and the huntsmen with the King's great hounds in leash.

Tristan froze as the hounds passed by, his heart beating thick and heavy in his throat. But he and Karherdin had chosen their positions with care, on the down-wind side of the track; and no breath of air carried their scent to the hounds.

After the huntsmen, came the King himself, riding among his nobles. And Tristan, watching between the tangled thorn branches, saw how his hair had greyed beneath the leather cap he wore, and how his face had aged and grown hard and heavy. But he passed on with all the rest; and behind him followed the Queen's maidens with her pages and cupbearers, riding in pairs. And last of all, riding with only Brangian and Perenis beside her, and the hound Bran running at her horse's heels, came Iseult the Queen; and instantly to Tristan it was as though another sun had risen and dawn was in the sky as well as sunset.

Beside him he heard Karherdin's whisper, "That is she?" And he nodded, and drew back his hand with the green reed he held, and sent it skimming like a dart into her horse's mane as she passed.

Iseult looked down and saw it clinging there; she glanced aside at Brangian; but never toward the thorn-

brake from which it had come. She plucked the reed
out and flicked it away as though it was a thing that had
come there by chance. She brought her horse to a halt,
and said to Perenis, "Ride ahead and beg the King to
make camp here in this pleasant place for the night, for
we have ridden far, and suddenly I am very weary."

And as her maidens began to turn back and gather
round her, she dismounted, and sat herself down on a
mossy tree-trunk beside the way, taking care to keep
the hound Bran close at her side.

Presently Perenis returned. "My Lord the King bids
me tell you that this is not a fit place to camp, for the
bushes grow so close that they would give cover to wolf
or enemy right into our midst. But a short way further
on there is open land and sweet water."

"What enemy does the King fear in his own hunting-
runs?" said Iseult. "No wolf will come in among the
camp fires; and if there is sweet water so close, let the
servants fetch it. Go tell the King that I am too weary
to ride even a short way further, and beg him to make
camp here."

So Perenis rode off again; and in a short while,
watching from his thorn thicket, Tristan saw the whole
hunting party coming back. He touched Karherdin on
the shoulder, and they slipped away further up the hillside; and there they lay watching the camp servants
setting up the striped tents and building the cooking
fires as best they could in the wooded and bush-grown

valley. Presently the smoke of the cooking fires rose from among the thorn trees, and torches began to flare in the deepening dusk; and Tristan heard the voices of the hunting party at their evening meal, and the struck notes of a harp.

When they had done feasting under the trees, the Queen rose and withdrew with her maidens to the crimson tent which had been set up for her near the thorn-brake from which the green reed had come. She sent her maidens away, all save Brangian, and when they were alone she said to her friend, "Set the torch over yonder, and high, where it will cast only a little shadow if anyone should happen to come into the tent. Now go after the rest, and if the King should come this way, tell him that I am already asleep and would not be wakened."

And still, among the thorn trees further up the hillside, Tristan waited, watching the camp below him until it was quiet, watching the glimmer of light from the Queen's tent, like a dim red rose in the shadows of the autumn night.

At last he rose, and went down towards it, silent as another shadow, while Karherdin lay among the thorn bushes and watched him go.

The cloak that hung over the entrance to the tent had been drawn aside, and he went in.

The old hound crouching at Iseult's side, sprang up at his coming, and came whining to rub its great shaggy head against his knees. And beyond, Iseult sat among the piled cushions, combing her hair that was red as hot copper in the smoky torchlight.

She said, "Put out the torch. It has served to guide you to me, and the moon is better for keeping secrets." And laid aside her silver comb and held out her arms to him.

FOURTEEN
ISEULT'S LAUGHTER

NEXT morning very early, with the autumn mist still hanging between the trees, Tristan and Iseult took their leave of each other. "Let me see that you still have my ring," Iseult said in the last instant; and Tristan showed it to her, hanging on a leather thong round his neck. She touched it. "Does your wife, this other Iseult that you told me of in the night, ever wonder why you wear a woman's ring about your neck?"

"She has had wisdom enough not to ask."

"She has more wisdom than I would have had in her place," Iseult said. "There, put it back inside your tunic; and remember always, that it will call me to you. —And remember also, the Geis that I set on you the last time we parted."

"I shall not forget. Anything that I am asked to do in your name, I will do, because I love you."

Then she took his face between her hands and kissed him; and he left her in the doorway of the tent and slipped out through the still sleeping camp and away up the hill to where Karherdin waited for him.

They said nothing as to the night, but set out towards the Steward's Hall. But they did not go all the way; Tristan had no wish to run any further risk of bringing trouble upon Dynas, his friend; and he had ordered Gorvenal and Karherdin's armour-bearer to meet them at a certain place with the horses, that they might all ride straight for the south coast of Cornwall.

Now by ill chance, one of King Marc's nobles, Beri by name, coming late to join the hunt, with several companions, chanced to see them on their way to the meeting-place. Karherdin's armour-bearer was dark, and of the same slight build as Tristan, and the man caught only a glimpse of him in passing, but recognized Gorvenal with him, and so thought that he was Tristan indeed, and called after him to halt, meaning to find out what he did in Cornwall and tell him of the hunt, for Beri was a friend to the Queen, though a somewhat foolish one.

When Gorvenal heard Tristan's name called after them, he said quickly to the young armour-bearer, "Ride! If they come up with us there may be sore trouble for us all!" And they struck spurs to their horses' flanks and broke into a gallop, the lead horses with them.

At their backs they heard the drum of hooves as Beri gave chase, and his voice, shouting above the hooves,

"Tristan! Tristan, would you be flying like a thief? Turn for your honour!"

"Ride!" said Gorvenal.

"Then in the name of the Queen Iseult, if you still love her!"

"Ride!" said Gorvenal.

The man's shouts grew fainter behind them, and at last they knew that they had shaken off both him and his company. Then they fetched a wide circle over the moors, and came back at last to the place where Tristan and Karherdin were waiting for them.

"You have been slow on the road, then," said Tristan.

"We were forced to be taking a long way round to shake off some men who rode on our trail," said Gorvenal. "They must have taken Bryn for you, for one of them—it was Beri, if I am not mistaken—called after him to turn, first for his honour's sake, and then in the name of the Queen if he still loved her."

And when he heard this, Tristan could have thrown up his head and howled like a dog, remembering his promise to Iseult, and knowing the harm that had been done all unwitting.

Meanwhile Beri, having lost the man whom he supposed to be Tristan, rode on to join the hunt deeply troubled, and contriving to get word with the Queen alone, told her how he had seen Tristan and called to him to stop, and how he had struck spurs to his horse and galloped off, refusing to turn even when called upon in the name of the Queen herself.

As she listened, the anger rose hot and most bitter within Iseult, and she remembered the promise that Tristan had made again to her only that morning. "He has broken faith with me," she thought. "And never could he have done that while he still loved me. —All his promises are false, and it is Iseult of the White Hands who holds his heart now."

Then she called Perenis to her, and bade him ride after Tristan and tell him that since he could forget his promises so easily, he had best forget all that had ever been between them.

Away rode Perenis, with a heavy heart. He knew where Tristan and Karherdin were to meet the others with the horses, and the road that they would take from thereon towards the south; and at the ford of a stream he came up with them and delivered to Tristan his message.

When he had heard it, Tristan said, "That is what I feared. Perenis, have you ever known me false to the Queen?"

Perenis shook his head.

"Then go back to her, and tell her this: that it was not I whom the Lord Beri saw, but an armour-bearer —see, there he stands, dark as I am and built much as I am—coming up with Gorvenal to meet me with the horses. He knew nothing of the promise between my lady and me. Say to her that if it *had* been I, I would have turned, for her sake, though there rode an enemy warhost on my trail."

"I will tell her," said Perenis. "But I am not sure if she will believe, for she is angry past clear listening, and past thought."

"Do the best that you can," said Tristan, "and bring me back her word. We will be waiting for you here."

So back again went Perenis, over the weary way, and found the Queen already gone to her tent, for by this time it was night. He told her faithfully all that Tristan had said; but she listened with a cold face turned aside. And when he had finished, she said only, "What did Tristan give you to tell me this story?"

"My Lady," said Perenis, "you are unjust, both to my Lord Tristan and to me!"

She looked long into his face, and laughed. "No bribe? Why, you simple soul, you believe him! Then go back and tell him that I do not believe so easily as you!"

"Lady, will you not send a kinder message?"

"Why should I? I do not care for faith-breakers," said she.

So back yet again went Perenis, on a fresh horse, but himself wearied to the bone; and came in the dark end of the night, to the place where Tristan and his companions waited, wrapped in their cloaks and with their horses tethered nearby.

Tristan listened, sitting where he had sat all night

beside the low fire that they had kept burning against wolves. And he bent his head onto his crossed arms and groaned.

"There is nothing more to be done," said Karherdin. "As soon as it is light, we will ride. If we can find a ship, we can be back in Brittany within five days. My sister is not so fair as the Queen of Cornwall, but she is kinder."

But Tristan was not hearing him at all. "I will go to her myself," he said. "I cannot leave her holding this against me."

Gorvenal said, "To go back is madness! It is to throw your life away!"

"No, for I shall not go in my own seeming. But if it *were* to throw my life away, still I could not leave her like this."

Gorvenal sighed. "Then we come with you."

"This is between myself and Iseult the Queen. There is no place in it for any other. Let Perenis go back now, and let the rest of you wait for me here; and if I come again, I come, and if I do not—then I wish you calm seas and safe roads back without me."

"And what of my sister?" said Karherdin.

"Comfort her as best you may. She will have need of it, but there is no comfort in me."

Then Tristan set about making his preparations. He took the old grey-hooded cloak that he had worn because it would blend into the country and not catch at any man's eye to be remembered afterward; and he whipped it with thorn branches and beat it between stones until it hung in rags; he rubbed into it wood-ash from the fire, and the staining lichen from the north sides of trees. And then he set to work with his dagger and some bits of old dry wood, to carve himself a clapper.

Gorvenal watched him like an anxious hound, and at last asked what he did.

"I make myself a leper's clapper."

"A leper's clapper?"

"It is a good disguise; few men care to tear a leper's hood from his face! Once before, remember, I went to her in this guise; now I go to her as a leper once again, and it may be that she will remember that other time."

And he set out, while the rest waited for him with anxious hearts.

He had far to go, for the hunting party were on their homeward way; and he must cover the distance cross-country and on foot. And it was long past noon when he heard the hunting horns gathering in the hounds far ahead of him, and came out onto the track in front of the hunting party. He stood beside the way, waking the dismal sound of his clapper as the head of the party passed by. Many of them threw him pitying or fearful glances, some swerved their horses aside, some tossed him a small coin; but he paid no heed to any, only stood there with his face hidden in his hood while they passed, until at last the Queen and her women came; and then he thrust forward—people barred his way, to guard the Queen, cursed him and shouted to him to go back. But he cried out to them that it had been promised him in a dream that if the Queen Iseult would but look into his face, he would be healed of his sickness.

"A leper's face? What sight is that for the Queen?" Brangian cried, thrusting her horse between them.

But the Queen said gently, "Surely it is a small thing to ask," gestured Brangian back and urged her horse towards him. And Tristan stood at her stirrup and looked up, his face hidden by his hood from all but her. She bent and looked into it, and he saw her eyes widen and her face change. She looked at him long and hard; and then she said, her voice ringing clear and sweet and cold as a glass bell, "I have looked. Now go your way, leper." And swung her horse aside.

"Not yet!" Tristan shouted.

"I have looked, and I am sickened with looking!" said Iseult, and then to the courtiers and the hunt servants nearest about her, "Drive him away! Away! Stone him if he will not go! I pray God I never see that face again!"

And then they were all shouting, "Off! Away with you, leper!" and stones from the track came spattering about him. But Tristan did not hear the shouts nor feel the stones. All that he heard, all that he felt, was Iseult's high cruel laughter, as he turned and blundered away.

Long after the hunting party was far behind him, he

seemed to hear that laughter in every bird-call among the trees.

It was nightfall when he came again to the three who waited for him by the stream, but they saw his face cut and bruised in the firelight, and they saw the look in his eyes, and they asked no questions.

So they returned to Brittany, and Iseult of the White Hands came out to meet them at the castle gate; and Tristan, swinging down from his horse, put his arms round her and kissed her as he had never done before.

And Iseult of Cornwall? She began as the months went by to regret most bitterly that she had driven Tristan from her in so cruel a way, and to think that maybe he had been telling truth after all. She grew to wish more than anything in the world that he might come back; and never any stranger came near her, but she hoped he might have brought her the ring, and never a man in a hooded cloak passed by, but her heart quickened and leapt into her throat at the thought that it might be Tristan himself.

But the months went by and the years went by, and the ring never came. And the face under the hood was never Tristan's. And her heart grew weary with waiting, and the Queen of Cornwall's crown was cold and heavy on her brow.

FIFTEEN

THE GARLAND AND
THE REEDS

*F*OR Tristan also, the months and the years went by. He had thrust Iseult of Cornwall from his life; and he had found a kind of peace that was sometimes almost happiness with Iseult White-hands. He had never told her of the other Iseult, but she had always guessed the meaning of the woman's ring that hung round his neck, and because she loved him she knew the rest without being told, and knew when he turned from the owner of the ring, and did all she could to heal the hurt, and yet could not help being glad that the hurt was there for her healing.

And then one day news came to Tristan that his father was dead, and war broken out among the Lords of Lothian; and he went to King Hoel and told him that he must return to his own country. The old King gave him three hundred warriors to follow him; and with Gorvenal, he went his way, leaving Iseult of the White Hands to wait for his return.

He was gone two years, dealing with the warring nobles and setting his kingdom to rights. And then, leaving Gorvenal behind to rule the land for him, he returned to Brittany.

He found that Hoel was dead, and Karherdin was now King. But the friendship between them was as strong as ever, and one day as they rode hawking together outside the city walls—they had left the old fortress of Carhaix long ago and returned to the Royal City, which was on the coast—Tristan said to his friend, "Now that you are King, you should be thinking of taking a wife." And watching the flight of his falcon, he thought how he had joined with the Cornish Lords in saying the self-same thing to King Marc—and what had come of it.

"You are not the first to tell me so," Karherdin said. "And indeed I know that you are right. But . . ."

"But it is still Gargeolain who holds your heart."

"Aye, so."

"Then go to her once more, as I did to the Queen of Cornwall—for see what a contentedly married man I am now," said Tristan, light and bitter. And far off against the sky, the falcon stooped upon the climbing heron, and a puff of dark feathers blew down the wind.

Karherdin thrust a hand into the breast of his tunic and brought out a great key and held it toward Tristan. "The thought has been in my mind often enough."

"The key to her Lord's castle?" said Tristan, looking at it.

"I bribed one of the servants long ago to get me a wax impression made, and my own smith did the rest."

"You have never used it?"

"Never, until now," said Karherdin. And they checked their horses, and sat turned in the saddle to look at each other. Then Karherdin laughed, and said, "Come with me, then. I went with you."

And in an ill moment Tristan said, "I will come." And they rode on together after the falcon that had made her kill.

A few days later, when the Lord Bedenis had ridden hunting as usual, Tristan and Karherdin rode out from the trees and drew rein before the gates of his stronghold. Karherdin was dressed in his gayest clothes, like a bridegroom, and on his sandy head he wore a garland of honeysuckle and wild columbine; but as they rode across the causeway that spanned the three great ditches of the stronghold, the fitful summer wind caught it from him and tossed it into the water. They came to the gates, and Karherdin beat upon them with the pommel of his sword; and a woman's voice cried out to know who was there; and women's braided heads came over the high battlements.

Karherdin called up to them, "Go tell the Lady Gargeolain that Karherdin the King is at her gates and begs to be let in."

Then the women exclaimed and twittered among themselves.

"The King! It is the King!" And one of them called down, "Gladly and gladly would our mistress welcome you in; but there is but one key to the gate, and the Lord Bedenis carries it always with him. And without it, we cannot let you in."

"There is another key," said Karherdin, "and it is here in my hand. Go and ask your mistress's leave that I may turn it in the lock and come in."

Then one of the women went, and came back in a while, and called down to him, "The Lady Gargeolain bids you turn the key in the lock, and enter!"

And when, bending down from his horse, he did so, the women within crowded round, gay as a flock of birds in their embroidered gowns, to bid him and Tristan welcome and draw them in and take their horses for tending, and lead them to the Great Hall. In the Great Hall, the Lady Gargeolain waited. And Tristan saw that she was little and gentle, she had a face like a flower and she would be as easily crushed as a flower, and he wondered what Karherdin saw in her. She held out her hands to the tall, gay, ugly man, and Tristan wondered how such little foolish hands could hold his strong and valiant heart; but then he saw the faces of both of them as they drew together, and he wondered no more.

But after the first moment, Gargeolain held the King off a little, trying to remember her courtesy to a guest, and said to her women, "Bide here and make our other guest welcome; tend to his comfort in all ways; it is long since my Lord Karherdin and I were last together, and we have many things to say to each other." Then, holding him still by the hand, she drew him away through an inner doorway.

Then the other women brought wine and fine white bread and scarlet strawberries in a bowl for Tristan, and he ate and drank, and made himself pleasant to them in all courtesy. And the time went by, and Karherdin and Gargeolain did not return. So he took up the little harp that someone had left lying on a cushioned bench, and tuned it, and played to them, waiting all the while for the inner door to open. And then when still the two did not return, he began to while away the time with tricks of the hand, for with being so much shut away, they were somewhat flitter-witted, and found such things enchanting. And amongst his other tricks, he took a handful of strong reeds from among the strewing-rushes on the floor, and breaking them off short, he skimmed the first at the wall so that it pierced the embroidered hangings and stood there quivering, just as he had skimmed his green reed for a signal into the mane of Iseult's horse, so long ago. Then he flicked a second reed after it, so that the tip went into the hollow end of the first, and a third into the hollow end of the second, and so on. And this he did many times, for the ladies never seemed to tire of watching the trick, which none of them had ever seen before, since Tristan alone had the knack of it.

At last, Gargeolain and Karherdin returned, with

their farewells all said. The horses were brought round, and he and Tristan took their leave, and went out from the castle, locking the gates again behind them. But Karherdin never thought of his garland floating among the water-weeds of the inner ditch, and Tristan never thought of the reeds clinging in the wall hangings of the Great Hall. And as they rode back toward the city they put up a roe deer, and though they had no hounds with them, they chased it, being in a mood for any foolishness; and so they wearied their horses to no purpose.

Now by an ill chance, the Lord Bedenis returned early from his hunting. He saw Karherdin's garland floating among the white water-buttercups, and knew that somebody had been that way. And when he came into his Great Hall, he saw the reeds hanging in the tapestry; and he knew that no one in all Brittany had the skill for that trick, excepting Tristan. He knew that Tristan was heart-friend to Karherdin the King, and he knew that it was Karherdin his wife had loved before she was forced to marry him. And Bedenis was no fool.

"Who has been here?" he demanded of Gargeolain.

"No one," she said. But she was deadly pale and trembled like a white poplar.

And the red fury rose in Bedenis so that he drew his sword, and seizing her by the hair, forced her to her knees, the blade-point at her throat. *"Who has been here?"*

"No one; indeed my Lord, no one!" she protested still.

He pricked her throat till a crimson fleck of blood stood on the white skin. "It was the King! Come, Lady, it was the King! Tell me, and I may spare that soft throat of yours!"

And at last she cried out in his face, "It was the King!"

He flung her from him, sprawling among her terrified women, and rushed out, shouting for fresh horses and his men to follow him. And soon they were crashing away through the forest toward the coast and the royal city.

Tristan and Karherdin heard the distant sounds of the hunt behind them. "Brother," said Tristan, "I hear horses, and I am thinking I know who hunts on our trail."

"Brother," said Karherdin, "I also hear horses; and I am thinking it is Death hunts on our trail." And he laughed, full throated, as he had laughed at most things in his life.

"Our horses are weary, and it's small hope we have of outriding this Black Hunt," said Tristan, "and for myself, I will not be taken from behind. If you are with me, let us find a good place to turn and fight our last fight."

"I am with you," said Karherdin.

And they spurred their horses to one last burst of

speed, toward the place where a limestone ridge cropped through the forest and would give them cover for their backs. And there they turned, sword in hand, to wait for the hunt to come up with them.

"I had thought to die in battle," Karherdin said, "a death for the harpers to make into a song. And I shall die with a jealous husband's sword in my throat. Life is a bad joke!"

"We can still make a battle to die in," Tristan said. "A small battle, but a red one—enough for a short song." And his hand tightened on the hilt of his sword, as Bedenis and his followers crashed into sight on the other side of the clearing.

The birds rose screaming from the tree-tops at the clash of weapons. It was twenty against two; but Tristan and Karherdin made their battle. Their horses were killed under them, and they fought on on foot. Then Karherdin, with three dead men about him, went down with a last defiant shout cut short by the red blood spurting from his throat; and Tristan bestrode his body and fought on alone. He saw Bedenis' face snarling before him and raised his sword for a great stroke; but he was growing slow with weariness, and another man's blade came in from the side under his guard; and took him in the groin. He stumbled to his knees and tried to struggle up again, that he might meet death on his feet; the sky above the tree-tops turned to a spinning black, and he knew nothing more.

When all was over, Bedenis with the few men left of his hunting party, rode grimly and heavy-hearted, home. He had avenged the insult to his house; but he had lost good friends in the fighting; and he had slain the King, and he knew that sooner or later he himself must be hunted down.

SIXTEEN

THE BLACK SAIL

NEXT morning, searchers from the city found Tristan and Karherdin lying beside their horses against the rocky outcrop, surrounded by the warriors they had slain before they were overcome. Karherdin the King was dead, and Tristan sore wounded, and seemingly with scarce a breath of life left in him.

They cut branches and wove them into rough hurdles, and carried them back to the city, one to lie in his own chamber in the high castle while Iseult of the White Hands bathed his wounds and sought to staunch the slow crimson bleeding; one to lie before the altar in the church, with candles burning at his head and feet.

Next day, Karherdin was buried with all the solemn pomp with which Kings are laid in their graves, while all Brittany mourned for him. And from far and wide the physicians whom the Princess Iseult had summoned came to try their skill for the healing of Tristan's wound. One after another they tried their remedies, and one after another they failed. Once again it was as it had been after his battle with the Morholt. The wound sickened and Tristan grew weaker day by day.

He knew that once again, there was only one person in the world who could heal him, and that was Iseult of Cornwall. But whether she could heal him or no, he longed for her; if need be just to see her face once more before he died; and the face of Iseult White-hands became like a stranger's that had no meaning. At last, he sent for Karherdin's armour-bearer—that same Bryn who had come with them on the last visit to Cornwall; and taking the ring from its thong about his neck, gave it to him. "Take this ring to the Queen of Cornwall; tell her how it is with me, and beg her to come to me quickly, for if she does not, then I must die. And when you return, if she is with you, cause the ship that carries you to show white sails; but if she will not come, then let the sails be black, for then it will be time to put on mourning for me."

So Bryn disguised himself as a merchant, and took ship for Cornwall; and he came to Tintagel and into the Queen's private apartments, under pretence of having jewels to sell that might interest her. When they were alone together save for Brangian, the Queen bade him show his wares if he had anything worth looking at.

"In truth," said he, "I have one jewel that you may find worth your looking at, Lady. It is this." And he held out to her the gold ring that she had given Tristan so long ago.

The Queen looked down at it in silence, and the blood drained from her face, leaving her white as snow, and then flooded back so that her cheeks blazed like fire, and her eyes were brilliant as a falcon's. "What message comes with this ring?" she said at last.

"My Lord begs you come to him, for he is sore wounded, and must die."

Then the fire drained from her cheeks and she was again as white as snow. "How does this come about?" she asked.

And the armour-bearer told her all the story.

"Wait," she said, "while I gather the things that I need." And to Brangian, "Bid Perenis have my horse waiting beyond the orchard, and a fresh horse for my Lord's armour-bearer. And meanwhile, give him food and drink. I shall not be long."

Brangian said, "Three horses, my Lady. You must let me ride with you."

"No," said Iseult, "for your life is here, and whichever way the wind blows, I do not think that it will blow me back to Cornwall again."

And so, at last, without a backward glance, Iseult of Cornwall left her husband and her country, her crown and her honour, and rode south with Tristan's armour-bearer, taking with her nothing but a little carved box containing the herbs and salves of her leechcraft. And it was not until the Court gathered in the Great Hall at evening, and her place beside the King's High Seat was empty, that the King or any man knew that she was gone.

Meanwhile, in the high castle above the city on the coast of Brittany, as the time drew near for Bryn's return, Tristan lay on his bed seeming like one already dead save for the life that still burned in his fever-brilliant eyes. And one thought ran like a caged and tormented thing round and round within him: would the sail of the ship, when it came, be white—or black? White or black? White or black?

Now Iseult of the White Hands had seen that the woman's ring was gone from about his neck; and as she sat beside him in the long nights while the fever raged through his body, she heard him talking and talking in the wild waking dreams of his sickness; and so she knew that he had sent for the other Iseult, and of the signal of the white sail or the black. And jealousy tore at her, for she thought, "I have been his loving and faithful wife these five years and more; and what has she done for him, this other woman with my name? What has she done for him save leave him without a heart in his breast? And yet now it is her he turns to, and he looks at me as though his eyes had never touched my face before."

And the days went by and the nights went by, and there were storms and then flat calms at sea that delayed the ship. And Iseult saw with an aching and terrified heart that waiting for the ship was the only thing that still held Tristan to life.

And then one morning when the first sunlight stole into the room, Iseult rose from her night-long watch beside the bed, and went to the window that looked toward the sea to feel the cool air on her forehead. And there, out on the blue water, a ship was heading in to harbour from the direction of Cornwall. And the sail was as white as the underside of a gull's wing.

Joy and grief welled up together within her; joy that the one person who could perhaps save Tristan was coming to him; grief that it was the woman he loved as he had never loved *her*. Her eyes were suddenly blind with bitter tears, and the joy and the grief fought each other within her so that she seemed filled with a kind of war.

She heard a faint movement from the bed, and Tristan's voice, so weak that it was only a whisper, asked, "What do you see out there?"

"I see a ship, far out but heading for the harbour."

"From what direction does she come?"

"From the direction of Cornwall."

There was another movement from the bed, sharp and agonized, and when she looked round she saw that he had fought up onto one elbow, and she saw the fear and the longing in his eyes. "Look again and tell me— what colour is the sail?"

And the cruel jealousy burst up in her, and for that

one moment she was filled with rage against him. And the words were spoken before she knew it, "I have no need to look again. The sail is black."

She saw the light go out of his eyes; and he fell back on the pillow and turned his face from her towards the wall. She ran to bend over him and heard him whisper, "Iseult! Iseult, why did you not come?" and knew that it was not her he called to; and as she put her arms round him and gathered him close, a great shudder ran through him, and she was left calling his name and clinging to him, and knowing that he was dead.

Her cries brought her ladies running, and then Tristan's armour-bearer; and then the Steward was there and the priest. Tristan's body was made ready for burial, and laid on a bier hung with white silk, and borne into the church, to lie where Karherdin had lain with candles at his head and feet.

The wind blew offshore all that day, and it was close to evening before the ship from Cornwall could enter harbour. And the first sound that Iseult of Cornwall heard from the city was the church bells tolling. As she stepped ashore she asked the first man she met, "Who do the bells toll for?" But every bell-beat fell like a stone upon her heart and she knew the answer before ever he told her.

"For the Lord Tristan, who lies in the great church yonder, waiting burial."

Bryn the armour-bearer would have come with her,

but she waved him fiercely back, and went forward alone. With her head held high as though it still bore the weight of a crown, she walked up through the mourning city, between the silent crowds that lined the streets. She looked neither to the right nor left, but followed the sound of the tolling bells, until she came to the church door, and saw the bier before the altar, and the candles at the head and feet, the clergy and the gathered nobles, and the woman silently wringing her white hands, her hair unbound in mourning, who stood close beside the bier.

She walked up the church, until she too stood beside the bier and faced the other woman across Tristan's body.

Then Iseult of Cornwall spoke, clear and cool under the tolling of the bell. "Lady, stand further off, I pray you; for I have the right to be nearest him. I mourn him more than you. I loved him more than you."

A murmur ran round the church, and Iseult of the White Hands gave her back look for look. "That, I doubt," she said, "but he loved you more than ever he loved me." And she stepped back and left the place closest beside him to the other woman.

Then Iseult of Cornwall stooped and drew aside the embroidered pall, and looked long and long into Tristan's face. "Love, you sent for me, and I came," she said, "I am too late to bring you back, but I can go with you, and so we shall be parted no more."

And she lay down on the bier, close beside him, and

put her arms about him and kissed him long and sweetly on the mouth. And with the kiss, her heart broke, and her spirit left her to go after his. And there were two bodies on the bier, where there had been one.

Iseult of the White Hands was torn with grief for her one moment of blind jealousy; and she caused Tristan and Iseult to be buried together in a noble tomb. But they were not left to lie there long, for when word of their deaths reached King Marc, he spoke no word of sorrow; but he took ship for Brittany, and with the Princess's leave, brought their bodies back to Cornwall; and there again they were laid in one grave side by side.

And out of Tristan's heart there grew a hazel tree, and out of Iseult's a honeysuckle, and they arched together and clung and intertwined so that they could never be separated any more.

It's still worth the risk?"

"Yes," she said solemnly. "It is."

Dr. Meade stood and looked down at Callie thoughtfully. "I promise you," he said again. "Your secret is safe with me."

Callie nodded.

"And there's something else I need to tell you—" he began.

Just at that moment, Titus opened the French doors. "Your assistant is here, sir. And he says you're needed at the stables. A new driver named Israel is asking to see you."

"Callie, I need to explain—" Dr. Meade began again.

But she wasn't listening. Her eyes were fixed on the figure at the top of the wide porch stairs.

For a moment, Hawk stood as still as a deer in a meadow glen, his eyes locked on hers. Then he walked slowly toward her along the stone-covered pathway through the formal gardens to where she waited.

Hawk stood before her without speaking. His gaze seemed to embrace her with the feel of the wild lands where they'd first met, with those eyes the color of New Mexico's purple skies, and skin the hue of its bronzed mesa sands.

"My assistant, Dr. Jones," the older doctor finally said to Callie. "I believe you've met." Then he quietly slipped away to see about his business with Israel at the stables.

Summer 2009